HIDDEN PLACES

Young widow Lauren and her son Scott have emigrated to New Zealand, where they inherit an unusual home set in a thermal park. Lauren keeps the park running smoothly for tourists, but struggles with the huge task. Desperate for help, her advertisement for assistance is answered by hunky Travis, and she believes her problems are solved. But there are major troubles ahead and important decisions to be made. Both love and deception will play a part in her dramatic new life.

CHRISSIE LOVEDAY

HIDDEN PLACES

Complete and Unabridged

LINFORD
Leicester

First published in Great Britain in 2006

First Linford Edition
published 2007

British Library CIP Data

Loveday, Chrissie
    Hidden places.—Large print ed.—
Linford romance library
    1. Widows—Fiction
    2. Hot springs—New Zealand—Fiction
    3. New Zealand—Fiction 4. Love stories
    5. Large type books
    I. Title
    823.9′2 [F]

    ISBN 978–1–84617–831–3

Published by
F. A. Thorpe (Publishing)
Anstey, Leicestershire

Set by Words & Graphics Ltd.
Anstey, Leicestershire
Printed and bound in Great Britain by
T. J. International Ltd., Padstow, Cornwall

This book is printed on acid-free paper

1

'I must have been mad to think I could make it work,' moaned Lauren as she chatted to the older woman.

'Brave, dearie, I'd say.' Mrs Campion leaned on the counter of her small grocery store and smiled at her new friend. 'Took some guts to come to a new country, right out here to the middle of nowhere. With your little lad as well. You deserve to make a go of it.'

'We were doing all right till that wretched Jarrett character left me in the lurch. Right out of the blue, he decides he's had a better offer. Two days later he's gone. Left us right in it.'

'I doubt he'll turn out to be much of a loss. Let's hope someone answers your advert. I'm sure they will. Who knows, pretty young lady like you. Have 'em queuing up in no time. Mark my words.'

'I wish. Still, I hope you're right. Well, I'd better get back. Thanks for the chat. How much do I owe you?'

'Twenty-nine dollars, love. Your aunt getting on all right?'

'She's OK, I suppose. Supposed to be coming out of hospital next week, but she's going to find it all a bit of a strain, I should think. We'll just have to see how she goes.'

'Such a worry for you. Your mother's sister, I think you said?'

'That's right. She had no-one else. There seemed nothing to keep us in the UK. Auntie Gwen needed us and so we came.'

Lauren picked up her shopping bag and walked back down the hill to her home. The lake rippled in the morning breeze and she watched birds skimming the emerald water that gave the area its name, Emerald Valley. It was such a beautiful place, she thought as she sighed, wondering if she would really be able to stay there.

It was so good for her little boy,

Scott. At six, he was convinced she could do everything and adored the life out here in a remote corner of New Zealand. Having a boat and a lake on the doorstep with plenty of fishing, his own dog for company and the summer to look forward to, must have seemed like paradise.

For Lauren, it had been a desperate decision. Her husband, Adam, had died four years ago. Following her mother's recent death, the offer from her aunt had come out of the blue, looking like a complete package for their salvation.

★　★　★

'Scott? Where are you?' Lauren called. There was no sign of the child. She didn't need to worry. It was all so safe here. He'd been playing with Pooch, her aunt's mongrel, outside the shop and had probably wandered back to their home. He'd had to learn to grow up rapidly over the past months.

When Aunt Gwen, her mother's

sister, had written to say she wanted to offer the two of them a home, it had seemed like the best thing ever. Gwen needed an urgent operation and in return for Lauren's help in looking after the park, their new life had become a reality.

Scott was sitting on the jetty outside Auntie Gwen's little café and gift shop. His feet were hanging over the edge, dabbling in the icy cold water of the lake.

'When will it be warm enough to swim?' he demanded to know.

'Maybe never. Not for me at any rate. The water comes down from the mountains and it's always pretty cold. But you may want to swim if the weather gets really warm.'

'I think it's funny that water doesn't get really warm with all those geysers and everything just across the lake.'

Auntie Gwen's rather unusual property serviced a small thermal park, typical of this area of North Island. Traditionally owned by the Maori people, the park had been developed by a company and was now managed by her aunt.

It was sited along the string of volcanos and other thermal phenomena which went from White Island out in the Bay of Plenty, right down beyond the volcanic Mount Ruapehu towards the South. Lauren was fascinated by the whole country, as much of it as she had managed to see so far.

It seemed strangely primeval in its way, as if it was still making its mind up which way it might develop. Huge vents of steam shot into the air at intervals and water pushed its way, boiling from the ground. There was also a huge cave with a hot water pool, deep in the base. Exotic ferns and tropical trees grew in the warm micro climate helping provide a magnet to attract tourists.

Their secret valley was hidden away from the major routes and so it needed the more determined adventurer to discover the amazing sights. Auntie Gwen's property was on the opposite side of the lake to the thermal area and as well as providing drinks, snacks and the usual souvenirs, ran the ferry taking the tourists to visit the site. There were also some letting rooms, though this side of the business had not been used for some months.

'Come on Scott. It's lunchtime. We need to be ready in case anyone arrives to visit the site this afternoon. I'll be needing your help.'

'OK Mum. I can drive the boat across the lake. No worries.'

'You most certainly can't. I'll need you to stay here and keep watch over Aunt Gwen's shop if I have to take anyone over to the other side.'

'When are we getting someone to help us?'

'When someone turns up, I guess. I put the advert in last week's paper, but nobody's replied yet. I want to get the shop and café organised before the season starts properly.'

Scott slipped his hand into his mother's. 'Don't worry, Mum. It'll be all right. Auntie Gwen will soon be home and then she can help out can't she? And soon, I'll be big enough to help with the boat and everything.' Lauren smiled.

★   ★   ★

It was only a couple of weeks later that their lives were to change dramatically, once more.

'Poor Auntie Gwen. She never deserved this,' Lauren sobbed to Mrs Campion.

'There, there dear. I know. It must be so hard for you. Coming to this wild place and your only relative going like that. But you've got new friends here. We won't let you down.'

'Thanks Mrs Campion. You're very kind. But I really don't know what we're going to go next. I sold up everything back home and we'd planned to make our home here with Auntie Gwen and help run her business.'

'It's all your business now, dear. She left everything to you, I understand.'

'Yes, yes, she did. But I don't know much about running it for working the park or anything. I've never been a business-woman.' Lauren was panicking slightly, at the thought of her inheritance. All the same, it could be a secure future for herself and her little boy, albeit a somewhat strange prospect. Though she had become fond of Auntie Gwen in the few short weeks since her arrival, she had always been a rather distant relation in all senses. Her demise was sad, but not the devastating bereavements she had suffered when her husband and mother had died.

'It could prove to be a little goldmine here,' Mrs Campion continued. 'You should develop the café and souvenir shop. Get the bed and breakfast side running again. The campsite's all set to expand along the road there. You could do all sorts. Boat hire. Water sports.'

'Steady on. I'm on my own here, don't forget. Nobody to help me. It's hard enough to ferry visitors across the lake, let alone do everything you're suggesting. I'm not wonder woman, you know.'

'You look pretty good to me. You wouldn't be Lauren Wilmshott, would you?' drawled a voice from the doorway.

'Lauren Wilmshaw, actually. Yes, that's me. How can I help you?'

She turned to look at the vision standing before her. Inexplicably, her heart began to pound. She forced herself to curb the desire to sit down heavily.

'Leyton Travis. Most folks call me Travis. I hear you're the one looking for help. I'm your man.'

'How do you do. Yes, I am looking for someone. This is Mrs Campion, by the way. Runs the grocery store down the lane.' Her voice was remarkably calm, in the circumstances. Her neighbour was staring unashamedly at him.

'Hello there, young man. I'd better get back. You OK now, Lauren? You want me to stay? I can give Jamie a call, if you'd like me to stay on awhile.'

'I'll be fine. Thanks again for stopping by. I appreciate your support. Hey, if you see Scott anywhere, can you ask him to come home?'

'Sure. Bye now.' The large, friendly woman left, glancing back at the handsome stranger she had just met. Now he would most certainly be an asset to Lauren and her new business. She wondered if he was married or attached to anyone. Young Scott could do with a strong man about the place, to show him the ropes. Teach him all the man things a boy should know about.

She hoped he would be satisfactory and possibly bring some new romance into Lauren's life. She was a lovely young woman, much too young to be a widow and too attractive to stay one for long. Leyton Travis, eh? If she'd been twenty years younger and unattached, she might even have made a play for him herself. She gave a chuckle. Even if she was a few years too old, looking didn't hurt anyone and boy and was he something to look at.

Lauren stared at the newcomer, taking in every detail of his striking looks. He was well over six feet tall, making her feel very tiny in comparison. He must have been a good eight inches taller than she was. She saw his warm brown eyes and felt immediately comfortable with him. Large and dependable were her first thoughts. His dark brown hair was slightly long and ruffled in the wind. He pushed it back from his face with a careless, slightly impatient gesture.

He was obviously used to the outdoor life and wore faded jeans and a heavy checked shirt. His hands were wide and capable looking.

'I'm sorry. I wasn't expecting anyone. Everything's been in such a muddle recently. I only just inherited the place. My aunt, the previous owner, well she died last week.' Her clear blue eyes felt as if they might allow some tears to escape if she wasn't careful and she blinked them away.

'I'm sorry. I could come back tomorrow. Or later in the week if it would help. I'm looking for summer work. I saw your advert in the paper and I was interested. Beautiful spot you've got here.'

'It is lovely. Quite an inheritance. Not exactly what I was used to before, I must say.'

'You're from England, aren't you?'

'Yes. I guess I still have the good old English accent. Not that you've got much of an accent yourself. Are you a local man?'

'Not really. I've travelled round a bit. I've lost most of the accent I may have had, at school overseas. But I was New Zealand born and bred. Now, perhaps you'd explain what my duties would be? If that is, we can agree that I may be what you're looking for.'

She swallowed, wondering how she would cope with such a physical male presence close by. She ran through the main chores that needed someone's help. The thermal park had passed only the minimum safety standards needed for tourists. There were a number of repairs needed before they could re-apply for this year's certificate.

Most of all, she needed someone who could handle the boat. The park itself could only be reached by boat, making it a very different place from most of the other attractions anywhere around.

'And you've been coping with all this on your own? As well as having to get over the loss of an aunt? You poor thing. No wonder you needed help so desperately.'

Unconsciously, he put a sympathetic hand on her arm as he spoke. She felt a dart of something akin to electricity rush along her arm beneath his strong fingers. 'How long have you been managing on your own?'

'Since my previous help left. About four weeks ago, while my aunt was in hospital. He walked out without any warning. Scott, my son, has tried to help, but he's only six and can't do more than help mind the shop. Besides, he's too busy learning to fish at the moment. I'm terrified he'll catch something. I wouldn't know what to do with it.'

'I could start right away, if you're interested.' Travis said, suddenly decisive. 'I've got all I need in the van. Just need somewhere to spread out my sleeping bag.'

'I have a room you can use. I'm afraid the pay isn't much. Not until I can sort out the accounts. You could have all your meals with us of course and the room is free.'

'Sounds ideal. Show me the way and I'll take a look over at the park. Looks pretty spectacular from here.'

'Shouldn't I see references, that sort of thing?' Lauren asked uncertainly. She didn't want to offend this most likeable man, but on the other hand she knew nothing about him. But if he'd heard her, he made no sign of acknowledgment. She gave a shrug. Apart from knowing she wanted him to stay, her instincts told her that he must be reliable. She was pretty desperate and besides, he was the only person who had applied for the job.

'Whose is the pick-up truck?' asked Scott, coming into the room. The six-year-old had inherited his mother's blond hair and blue eyes and had an even greater sprinkling of freckles over his face.

'Belongs to a Mr Travis. He may be coming to work for us. I think he must be looking at his room, at the moment . . . ' her voice tailed off.

'Wicked! Does he know about boats and fishing? Can he tell me why I never catch anything?'

'I really don't . . . '

'What bait are you using?' asked the man, as he came back into the room. 'You must be Scott. And I'm Travis.' He held out a large hand to the child.

'Hi,' said the little boy, slightly shy of the large man. He'd had very little contact with any man, since his father had died. He put his little hand into the visitor's hand and shook it formally. Lauren watched as their eyes met. She saw an instant trust light her son's face, as they began to chat easily about fishing. Was it merely a child's innocence or did it suggest the stranger was really trustworthy?

From everything she had seen so far, Travis looked as if he might be the answer to quite a few of her current problems. Even Pooch had turned up and was currently making a huge fuss of the man. One should certainly trust a dog's instincts, she decided, crossing her fingers. Travis could be everything she needed in her life at this time.

2

It took several weeks before all the legalities were completed. At last, Lauren's legacy was all signed and sealed. Auntie Gwen had left everything to her, property, business and a small sum of money. During the weeks of waiting, she worked hard to get the house cleaned and freshened up with paint.

She was allowed to keep the business running between times and so the park was managed as usual. Travis was indeed turning out to be a huge asset, apart from being such a pleasure to have around the place. She enjoyed watching his powerful frame, as he worked. House or garden, he seemed willing to turn his hand to anything that needed doing.

He mended various safety fences in the park and made new warning signs for any part he considered even remotely unsafe. The odd few tourists had visited but the main season was still some time off. Once Scott was in bed, they spent their evenings companionably watching TV, listening to music and reading.

She was intrigued by the man. Though he liked to give the impression of being a simple labourer, she soon discovered he was extremely well read and knew a great deal about all kinds of music. She tried to prise information from him about his past, but he would not be drawn.

'I like to live for the here and now,' he said enigmatically. 'The past is gone and there's nothing one can do about it. But you can always hope to shape the future.'

'But you surely learn from the experiences of the past, she pressed. 'Use that to shape your future.'

'Sometimes perhaps. But one never knows what is waiting round the corner to make the future. You must know that from what you've told me about your own past.'

'I often play the game of 'what if' ... I wonder how different actions might have changed things.'

'Exactly my point. One can waste too much time wishing, wondering how you might change things. But you didn't. And you can't spend the rest of your life thinking that you won't let Scott do anything in case something dreadful happens. Drive you both mad in no time flat. Stop him turning into a balanced adult at the same time. Now, I think I'll make a drink and then turn in. You want something?'

'Please. I'll have a de-caff coffee. Anything stronger and I won't sleep. And, despite what you say, that is learning from past experience.' Lauren scored her point. He laughed and held a hand up in mock surrender.

'Message received.' He went into the kitchen and she heard the comforting rattle of kettle and mugs and felt grateful to have another adult human in the house. Especially this particular one. The now, totally devoted Pooch, followed him like a shadow. Whatever the man's background, she was delighted to accept the here and now of his presence.

* * *

Lauren and Travis took turns to fetch and carry Scott to the school bus, depending on their chores for the day. The child himself was longing for the school holidays to begin in three weeks' time.

'We'll all have to be working much harder once the tourists begin to come. Our present one or two trips a day across the lake will be nothing. We hope there will be people coming every few minutes. And I hope we shall be doing good trade in the shop,' Lauren told him, when he asked if Travis would go fishing with him every day.

'We'll manage a bit of time,' Travis promised. 'But I'll need your help to keep everything running smoothly. What do you say?'

'That'll be great. What sort of things might I need to do?'

'Oh, handling tickets. Checking the boat's fuel is always topped up.'

'I don't want him handling diesel oil. It's too dangerous,' Lauren said anxiously. Travis gave her a warning glance, but his mouth softened into an understanding smile.

'He won't have to. But he's quite capable of checking levels. He'd be looking at the dials on the boat and dipping the rod into the bulk tank. I'll need to know when we need to order more. And I'm sure he'll be able to keep a tally on the postcards and other stock. Be a real help to his mum.'

'Course I can,' Scott beamed. 'I can count really well and I can read quite a bit too now.'

Lauren smiled at the two males and ruffled her son's hair. Travis was staring at her with a faint smile on his face. She felt slightly unnerved and glanced away, lowering her eyelids. She felt her cheeks colouring slightly. It was a long time since any man had looked at her that way.

'Hopefully, our cash flow will improve and I shall be able to pay you a decent wage. You've been very understanding all these weeks.' Travis had taken only the barest minimum in the way of wages, willing to help out until they were up and running. The small amount of money left by Auntie Gwen was disappearing alarmingly, as they spent it bringing the business up to scratch.

'I'm quite happy,' he insisted. 'You look after me very well. Excellent food on the table. Place to sleep. What more could I want?'

'I don't understand your motives though. You must have a life somewhere away from here. I mean, there's nothing much to keep you here.'

He stared at her and drew in a deep breath. 'It's a very beautiful place. There's a sort of peace here that's hard to come across anywhere. I feel happy here. Relaxed. The company's good and the locals are all friendly.' His eyes met hers in a steady gaze. She wondered if his words had some hidden meaning, but quickly came back to earth. How could there be anything more? She was almost thirty and had a small son. He was simply a very nice man trying to be pleasant.

'Well, I'm more than grateful to you.' He looked pleased as he touched her arm gently. She stared at his long fingers, fascinated. He moved them away, as if becoming conscious of the intimacy of his small gesture.

'Reckon I'd better go and make that check on the fences on the pink terrace. Looked a bit dodgy to me. Want to have everything just so for the safety guys next week.' Though it was a Saturday, work continued as usual.

'And I'd better find the time to read through the rest of my first aid stuff before next week. My test is getting pretty close. I'm dreading it.'

'You'll be all right. Bright lady like you will sail through. No probs.'

'Why do you have to do a first aid course?' asked Scott.

'Make sure I can cope if anyone gets injured. I've already had one day at the centre and next I have to attend for a few more hours tuition and then write the answers to a test.'

'I think it's silly. We can get a doctor if anyone's hurt.'

'Takes a while for a doc to get all the way out here. Your mum'll have to know what to do while we're waiting. Can make all the difference to someone living or dying.'

'If she'd known first aid, would she have been able to stop my dad from dying?' the child asked. Pain flicked through her eyes. She tried to speak firmly, without the catch in her voice that usually accompanied the reply to Scott's innocent remarks about his late father.

'I don't think so love. Your dad died in a road accident. A very bad one.

Nobody could have saved him. Now, let's get moving you guys. Lots to be done.' She needed activity to get away from the ache that the memories brought with them.

'You coming over with me, Scott?' asked Travis, eying Lauren as if trying to decide the best course to follow.

'OK. If that's OK with you, Mum?'

'Keep to the tracks. No walking on the rocks. I can do without burned feet and trainers.'

'Course not. I know all the rules.'

'Don't worry, Lauren. I'll keep him in line or he'd better watch out.' He made a mock run towards the little boy and caught him up in his arms. 'I know exactly what to do with bad lads who don't do as their mum tells them.' The child shrieked with laughter at the man-handling. It was exactly what he had been missing, Lauren could see.

'OK. I'll see you later. I'll make us something special for supper. Maybe some cakes for dessert.'

'Sounds great,' Travis said with a broad grin.

She watched the man and boy as the little boat glided across the lake. Pooch sat high in the bows, watching the land on the other side of the lake approaching. He had lived here all his life and knew every inch of the strange thermal park.

The trees grew high up the banks on either side, making the whole valley a sheltered, secret place. It was so beautiful, she thought dreamily. A flock of birds skimmed over the water, making ripples when their wings caught the water as they snatched at flies.

No wonder Auntie Gwen had stayed on to make her home here, even after her own husband had died. There was a tranquillity that existed here, probably more than anywhere else in the world. With a small sigh, she turned to go back into the shop to complete the orders for stock.

She was engrossed in some catalogues when she heard a vehicle pull up on the gravel outside the garden. She stood and looked out of the window. It was much too late in the day for any tourists to be arriving.

Two men were sitting in a large, flashy looking car. She thought one of them might be in uniform, but it was impossible to tell. One of them got out and stood arms folded, looking around. The other man remained in the car, his uniform clearly visible. What on earth could a chauffeur-driven car want at her remote place?

She went to the door and stood outside. The man looked towards the shop and seeing her standing, began to walk slowly towards her. For some unknown reason, she gave a shiver of apprehension. Travis was out of reach, but she knew she could ring the large bell outside if she needed him to return. It hung there so that they could summon the boat to return if needed, matching the one on the other side, used by visitors if they worried they may be stranded.

'Mrs Wilmshaw?' he asked. He was dressed expensively, in a suit that would have been more appropriate in a city office rather than a country thermal park.

His hair was neatly cut and greying slightly at the temples. The effect was spoiled by the gold chain he wore at his throat and another, heavier one at his wrist. A Rolex watch adorned the other wrist and she also noticed a diamond ring on one finger.

She could smell his expensive cologne and knew she disliked him immediately. Lauren felt at a total disadvantage in her worn jeans and scruffy T-shirt. Unconsciously, she smoothed her hair behind her ears as if trying to tidy it.

'Who's asking?' she replied cautiously. He took a card from a slim gold case and handed it to her.

Charles Andrew Development & Acquisitions she read.

'I'm sorry. I don't understand. Are you selling something?' She had no spare capital for investments, other than what was essential for her own property.

'Buying, I hope. I'm interested in purchasing your lot. Shop, café, site. The whole piece of land.'

'Then you've had a wasted journey. It's not for sale.'

'I'm prepared to make you a very generous offer. I gather you've recently inherited the place. Pretty run down, I'd say. Nothing here going to make you a decent living. What I'm offering will enable you to find a nice little place somewhere and still have money left over, plenty for you and your young son to live on. Tempting offer. I'd advise you think about it before dismissing it entirely.'

'How do you know about my son?' she retorted angrily. 'As I said, it is not for sale. Now, if you'll excuse me, I have work to do.'

Angrily, she turned away from the odious man and went back inside. She felt a tremor of anxiety rush through her, realising he had obviously done some research. He knew about Scott and also that she had recently inherited the property. She closed the door firmly, holding her breath and praying he went away. To her alarm, he followed her inside. She cursed herself for failing to drop the lock on the door.

'At least you should hear my offer,' he said in oily tones, smiling at her in a way that was supposed to win her over.

'There's nothing you can say that would interest me. Now, if you'll excuse me, I need to call my son and his companion back for supper.' She pushed past him slightly nervous and rang the bell vigorously. She hoped Travis would hear it and respond quickly. She saw Scott dance up to the top of the hill and wave.

She made beckoning motions and soon, the large, comforting figure of Travis appeared. He could see the car parked alongside the building. He gathered up his tools and trotted quickly down the slope to the boat.

Charles Andrews watched the panto-mime with a degree of amusement. With a wry grin, he spoke again. 'You need have no fears, madam. I am not a violent man. Not personally, that is. Merely a businessman interested in helping you to a better future.' The look in his eyes carried a thinly-veiled threat and Lauren shivered. He contin-ued, 'I'm speaking of a large sum of money, as I said. A very generous offer in the circumstances. You may like to give my office a call to learn more. You have the number.'

He turned, leaving the waft of expen-sive aftershave in his wake. Everything about him shouted money. Ostentatious money. His every word also seemed to suggest menace. Threats.

He stopped at the doorway and turned back. 'I should perhaps also make it clear. I always get what I want, eventually. Only if I'm kept waiting for too long, my offer goes down with each day. It would be a pity to see this place go for so much less than it's true worth.'

Angrily, she tossed the card into the drawer and shut it firmly. She would not sell her inheritance. It would be so disloyal to Auntie Gwen for one thing. Besides, this was going to be her future, hers and Scott's. And what was this man doing here on a Saturday evening? It was certainly not the time that conventional folk did business. She watched him disappear up the narrow road and then turned to look at the lake. Travis and Scott had almost reached the landing stage and she went towards them, grabbing the rope he tossed easily to her.

'What's up?' he called. 'Anything wrong?'

'No. I was worried for a moment though. I just thought it would be good to have you over this side.'

'Who was the visitor?'

She shook her head, warning him to say nothing.

'Sorry if I interrupted your work.'

'We were all but done, weren't we Scotty?' He rumpled the boy's hair affectionately. 'Getting to be quite the handyman, this one,' he said.

Scott beamed with pleasure. 'I actually hammered in lots of nails and only hit my thumb twice,' the child said proudly. 'And I never cried.'

3

'That sauce you made with the pasta was simply fantastic,' Lauren said when they finally settled down. Travis had insisted on cooking the meal. The supper was cleared away and Scott safely tucked up in his bed. 'And the brownies were certainly a big hit. I've never seen Scott tuck in quite so heartily. In fact, all in all, I'm beginning to feel quite inadequate.'

Travis grinned. 'You're looking pretty fine to me,' he said. 'So, what was behind all the bell ringing this evening?' When he tried to ask her before, she shook her head, not wanting to talk about her visitor in front of Scott.

'Some creepy guy came to make an offer for Auntie Gwen's business. My business. He followed me inside and I didn't feel at all comfortable. I'm sorry to be a coward, but I felt very threatened in some strange way.'

'You'd better tell me exactly what he said. And what did you say his name was?'

'Charles Andrews.' She saw Travis's expression change. His brown eyes suddenly hardened and their colour seemed to intensify. His mouth was set in a grim line.

'Tell me exactly what he said.'

'That he wanted to make me an offer for the business, house and everything. A generous offer. If I waited he would get less generous and eventually he would get the place anyhow. At a knock-down price.'

'And he said all this with no witnesses?'

'Course there were no witnesses. I was alone, as you know.'

'It sounds very much like a threat. But, as he was careful to make it all with only your word against his, we have nothing to fight him with.'

'Hey, hang on. Aren't you getting a bit dramatic here? What's with the idea of fighting anyone? He made an offer. I refused. He tried a bit of play-acting to make me change my mind. He is not going to succeed.' Her mouth set in determined line.

'I hope not,' Travis said with a worried tone to his voice.

'Do you know this man?' Lauren asked suddenly.

'I er . . . I know the name,' was his rather terse reply. 'Now, a drink for you? I need an early night. Lots to do tomorrow. And Lauren, in future, I don't want you in the shop alone with the door unlocked.

'If I'm away or over the other side, you lock the door. Right?'

'I think you're overreacting. I'm not scared, really. Besides, what about customers? They have to come into the shop. That's what it's all about for heaven's sakes. Besides, what's he going to do to me?'

'You may not want to think about it. Believe me. This man can be very dangerous. He has some very unpleasant friends. I don't want you taking any risks.'

Travis went to make their evening drinks, as usual, leaving her with a mixture of emotions. She had felt a tremor of fear at his words, but she also knew a sense of comfort at his apparent care for her safety. It seemed a long time since anyone really cared about her. Here was this relative stranger making a whole heap of noise about taking care and protecting her. It felt very nice, she had to admit.

Immediately, she felt a sense of disloyalty to her late husband. After all, it was partly her fault that the accident had happened. If she'd remembered to do all the shopping properly that morning, Adam wouldn't have needed to go to the local shop. The child may not have run out in front of him and caused him to swerve into the lorry. She shuddered as the familiar feeling shook her every time she thought of it. Travis was standing behind her, holding the cups of coffee.

'I reckon that shudder was another of those 'what if' thoughts.'

This man was just too observant, Lauren told herself. She should be careful. He'd be reading her entire mind next. He set the mugs down on the table next to her and rested his hand on her shoulder.

Flames licked through her body at his touch and she closed her eyes, trying to come to terms with the feelings that were beginning to rage through her each time he touched her.

'Relax Lauren. I'll look after you. I promise.' She smiled up at him, once more feeling small and relatively vulnerable beside him. Was it merely his masculine aura that provoked such a response? 'You've got a very lovely smile, you know. You should do it more often,' he said gently. He drew in a breath as if he intended to say more, but he let it go and sat down in his own chair and picked up his drink.

'Thanks Travis,' she mumbled. She cleared her throat. 'But you are scaring me. Why should I need looking after? I've had to manage on my own for a long time now. Who is that Charles whatever his name is? You sound as if you know him and as though you are frightened of him in some way.'

'You do have an imagination, don't you? Why are you so afraid of being looked after, as you put it?'

'I guess I'm not used to anyone worrying about me any more. And I don't know why you should think it has to be you doing the worrying. You have no obligation to me or Scott.'

Her cheeks coloured again and she looked down as if trying to concentrate on the coffee swirling in the mug. He leaned over and placed a finger under her chin, lifting her face to allow their eyes to meet.

'You're a very lovely woman, Lauren. You have taken me into your home without really questioning my own motives for being here. I'm grateful.'

Lauren's heart was pounding in a way that rendered her totally speechless.

She felt her breath catching in her throat, drying her mouth so that she was unable to say a word. She tore her own eyes away from his gaze and somehow managed to set her cup down with trembling fingers and moved towards him.

'Travis, I . . . ' she almost croaked, holding out her arms towards him.

'I want to kiss you, Lauren. But it's wrong. Right here and now, it's wrong. I'm sorry.' He rose from his seat and left the room. She was making an utter fool of herself. How could she possibly have believed someone like Leyton Travis could be interested in her, as a woman? She was nothing more than his boss. Would she never learn?

All the same, she hoped she hadn't ruined the possibility of his staying here for the foreseeable future. With the veiled threats and Travis's reaction to her visitor, she needed him to stay. At last, she dragged herself out of her chair and picked up the two congealing cups of coffee, took them into the kitchen and flung them down the sink.

She caught a movement outside the window and frightened, was about to yell for Travis. She mustn't she told herself. It was probably just an animal. She stared, as Travis's head and shoulders came into view. He must have gone outside for air, she realised. He'd wanted to escape from her clutches and had gone outside.

She closed her eyes, wishing that this evening had never happened. She went to bed and tossed around, knowing sleep would be slow in arriving.

What little sleep Lauren had managed, left her feeling dull and heavy the next morning. Of Travis, there was no sign. Feeling a sense of panic, she rushed to the side window and saw to her relief that his van was still parked outside.

She glanced around wondering if he was still in bed, but as that would have been most unusual, she discounted the idea. Scott appeared rubbing his eyes. He slumped into his seat at the table, unaware of anything, even that his cereal bowl wasn't in its usual place.

'Where's Travis?' he muttered, reaching for the packet of cornflakes and beginning to tip out a pile of flakes on to the tablecloth.

'Scott, what are you doing?' snapped Lauren. 'Concentrate will you?'

'Where's my bowl? I thought it was ready for me, as usual. At least I didn't pour milk on,' he said with a grin as he began to munch the cereal directly from the table.

'Get your bowl and eat properly.'

'Then can I go out with Travis?'

'We'll see. I'm not sure where he is. He may have gone out already.' She busied herself with scrambling eggs and put bread into the toaster, all the time looking out of the window in the hopes of seeing him. She still hadn't quite made up her mind about what to say to him. Mostly, she was in favour of saying little, pretending nothing had happened. It wasn't so far from the truth after all. Even the recognition that she could look at another man was most disturbing. It had never happened since . . . well, since Adam had died.

'Where did those flowers come from?' Scott asked suddenly.

'What flowers?' she murmured following her son's eyes to the dresser. There was a bunch of tight rosebuds, clumsily arranged in a glass tumbler. Travis must have left them. Her heart thumped with relief and she gave a tight little smile. 'I expect Travis must have found them and brought them in.'

'I think they might have been growing over the lake. I noticed something yesterday before you rang the bell for us to come back. Wonder why he went all the way over there just to pick a few old flowers?'

Lauren didn't answer. She smiled to herself. Whatever his reason, she was delighted that he had done it. When he finally came in for breakfast, her good humour was restored and she was able to chat normally, as if the small incident had never happened.

'Thank you for the flowers,' she told him. 'That was nice of you.' He smiled at her, his entire face seeming to light up. His eyes softened and took on the gentle look she was beginning to love. The realisation of her ridiculous thoughts hit her. Love. What was she thinking of? Automatically, she served breakfast.

Once she had organised everything in the kitchen she went outside and watched as Scott and Travis set off for the other side of the lake. She locked the doors as he had instructed and finally sat down with her first aid books to try and learn her notes. But she took in nothing. The words flowed before her eyes like leaves blowing in the wind. Love. Travis. Love. Random words came and went.

He was probably a dangerous man to love. It was utter folly to even consider a future of any sort with such a man. He was wanderer. Why else would he have come here, to this remote place? He would leave again, probably very soon. She should never have feelings for a wanderer. She had been feeling vulnerable and the experience of someone being such a good friend . . . such a sort of father to her son, was making her weak and foolish.

'I'm sorry, Adam,' she whispered. 'How could I even think I was beginning to love someone else.' Tears came to her eyes. Whatever happened, she must make sure that Scott wasn't becoming too attached to anyone else, especially a man. Especially a man like Travis.

He would disappear from their life as quickly as he had come into it. She tried again to concentrate on her books. Several times she looked out, thinking she could hear cars outside. But there were few tourists about at this time of year and nobody was visiting.

Near lunch time, she made a pot of soup and left it simmering until Travis and Scott returned. She heard the bell ringing over the other side and looked to see Scott waving as the little boat motored across the lake. The dark green waters parted in front of the white bows and left a trail of white behind.

'Hi Mum. We've had the best morning. Travis showed me how to fix the railings deep into the ground and how to cut back some of the bushes. Isn't it amazing how they can grow so huge in places that are so hot?' He prattled on without stopping. Scott's personal hero was standing with a lazy smile on his face as he watched the two of them.

'Whoa there,' Travis cut in, when Scott stopped for breath. 'How about washing your hands and then maybe we can eat some of that wonderful-smelling soup your mum's been making?'

'I gather Scott's been having fun,' Lauren said with a slight edge to her voice. 'It's very good of you to take so much time with a child. I'm sure he really appreciates it. I hope it hasn't been too much of a chore.'

'Lauren? I love being with Scott. He's a great kid. It's no sort of chore at all. My pleasure.'

'All the same. I'm not sure it's a good idea to spend so much time together. He'll really miss you when you move on.' She concentrated on stirring the soup and splashed her hand when she was a little too vigorous. She ran it under the tap and patted it dry.

'Are you giving me the sack?' asked Travis curiously. 'Only I assumed I was set here for a good long time. Is there something wrong?'

'I just don't want Scott getting too reliant on you. He's had to cope for most of his life without a man around. I'd hate for him to become too fond of you and then have it all taken away again.'

'You're his mother. I have to abide by what you say. But I think you're making a mistake. I have no plans to move on.'

'Maybe so. But I have to look out for my son. You must want more out of life than acting as a labourer. You're well read. Cultured. Don't you miss all the things a city can give you? It's positively primitive out here. Just the most basic things in life.'

'This place is a kind of paradise, in my opinion,' Travis said calmly. 'An oasis in a largely crazy world. Have no doubts, if I thought I could stay here forever, I might gladly do that.'

'I see. Well, I don't know quite what to say. I still think you'd soon get bored.'

'I doubt it. But you're right to some extent. I suppose I can't really say I'm going to stay here forever. I do have other commitments. All the same. With today's technology and all . . . ' his voice tailed off and he looked thought-ful. Lauren looked at him curiously. He really was something of an enigma. 'Actually,' he continued, 'I was going to mention it to you. I do need to go away for a day or two. I don't like leaving you at all, but it shouldn't take long to sort out a few things. Is it OK with you if I go off tomorrow? And then I'll be back well before the weekend.'

'Of course,' she agreed with a sinking

heart. Would he even bother to return, she wondered? 'You've had almost no time off since you arrived here.'

'That's unimportant. But I want you to promise me that you will lock the doors at all times and don't let Scott out of your sight.'

'What was that you said about giving him the opportunity to do his own thing?'

'I know. But things have changed slightly. I'll make sure everything is secure before I go and you keep your cell phone handy at all times. Get used to having it in your pocket. Here. Give it to me. I'll put my number in it so you can call at any time.'

'That's not a deal of use if you're somewhere miles away.'

'I can always get a plane back. You must just have noticed there are several light craft landing on the lake every day.'

'What is it you know about this man? For heavens sake. He only called in at the shop and he was perfectly civil. Not nice, but civil.'

'What does civil mean?' asked Scott from the doorway. Travis explained. They sat at the table, eating soup and the man spoke again to the boy.

'Look here, Scott, I'm afraid I have to go away for a couple of days. Three at the most. You'll look after your mum for me, won't you?'

'Why do you have to go away?' moaned Scott. 'Just when it's my holidays.' He scrubbed at his eyes which had begun to look a trifle damp.

'I have a spot of business to look after. I'll bring some stuff from the big bad city, too.'

'What sort of stuff?' he asked, his interest aroused. 'You promise you will come back, won't you?' the boy asked.

'Course. Now, if you've finished, how about we do some more fixing around the place?'

Scott's questions echoed the thoughts in Lauren's own mind. Would he really come back? However much she tried not to, she knew she minded a great deal. As he packed up his things the next morning, she felt as if something more than a few clothes was going with him. He leaned down to her cheek and kissed it briefly. He turned to Scott and picked him up, tossing him over his shoulder in a great flurry of laughter.

'Look after your mummy for me,' he called as he got into his van. He gave a wave and disappeared round the corner.

'He will come back, Mummy, won't he?' asked Scott anxiously.

'I certainly hope so, love,' she said quietly.

4

'Your good looking bloke gone away, has he?' asked Mrs Campion the next morning.

'Just some business he had to see to. He says he'll be back before the weekend.'

'That's good. We can do with a bit of decent male talent around here.'

'Mrs Campion.' Lauren laughed. 'You should be ashamed of yourself. He's certainly quite an asset though, I have to admit. Almost too good to be true.' Her eyes clouded slightly and she looked away, pretending to be studying the stock in the freezer. What if he didn't come back? What would she do? There hadn't been a single other applicant from her advert and well, Travis was everything she could possibly have wanted.

'You heard the news, love?' the kindly

woman was saying. Lauren shook her head. 'They say there are big changes ahead. This whole valley's gonna be developed. They're already building new chalets down the back there and someone's trying to buy up every scrap of land they can. There's talk of camping sites and even a huge luxury hotel.'

'Do you know who it is?' Lauren asked, a cold shiver running through her.

'No idea. Some big shot developer from Auckland, they say. Shame really, though trade should pick up a bit. Such a lovely place this. Still, can't complain, I guess. At my age, it would be good to know I'm secure in me old age.' She paused and looked worried as if a new thought had struck her. 'I guess they might build new shops and even a restaurant. That could rubbish both of us, couldn't it?'

★ ★ ★

Lauren was troubled and worked at her chores silently for most of the day.

Aware of Travis's parting words, she made Scott stay close by her. He was cross and wanted to be out doing stuff as he put it and not hanging around his boring mother.

'I need you to count all sorts of stock for me. Could you do that? Postcards first and then the chocolate bars. If there are more than fifteen of any one sort of chocolate, you can choose which one you'd like.'

'I could have one anyhow,' he said grumpily. 'If you don't know how many there are, I could always say there's one less.'

'Oh, no, young man. I know exactly what there should be and I'll know if you get it wrong.'

The banter went on for some time before he settled down with a pad of paper and a pencil. He carefully copied the names of each type of bar from the wrappers and then began to count them. Lauren worked on her accounts and wrote out some orders for more stock. Every time she heard wheels go along the road, she glanced up, half hoping it was Travis returning. Nobody at all visited and for two whole days, not even an interested hiker came by. When Friday dawned, she was hoping that this would be the day for her helper's return.

'Post's here,' yelled Scott. 'Shall I get it?'

'OK. Thanks. Lock the door when you come back.' The child had got used to her obsession for locking everywhere, even though at first he'd complained bitterly. Pooch barked as the mailman drove off and he bounded in with the little boy.

'We got a big fat letter here and a boring looking brown one. And some bills, I think. They usually are when they have those little window things in them, aren't they?'

'You can open the big one,' Lauren told him, as she recognised yet another catalogue. She turned over the boring looking brown envelope and ripped along the edge.

Dear Madam, she read. Further to our discussion last week, I am pleased offer you the sum of . . .

'Cheek,' she burst out. 'Five thousand dollars less than he offered last week and I told him clearly I wasn't interested in selling anyway.' She tore up the letter angrily and tossed it in the rubbish bin.

'What is it?' demanded Scott. 'This looks good. They've got some terrific stuff in here. Can we buy some?'

'Maybe. Nothing's up. Just some silly man who doesn't take no for an answer.'

'Is Travis back today? Only it's nearly the weekend and he said he'd be back for the weekend.'

'I don't know. Maybe.' She too, really hoped to see the van turning into the car park and the comfort of his presence. He seemed to inspire confidence and however little she really knew about him, she felt she could trust him completely. She tried to concentrate on her work and studying for her first aid examinations, but it seemed impossible.

'Let's go and take a look over the lake,' she said at last. She needed something more physical to do and Scott needed some fresh air and exercise. They locked the doors and went down to the little jetty. The small passenger boat was moored alongside and she fished in her pocket for the key to start it up. She switched on the ignition but nothing happened.

'You have to pull out that knob,' Scott informed her.

'I did,' she muttered. 'Maybe I needed to warm it for a bit longer. Diesel engines could be temperamental but this one was usually so reliable. 'It's no good,' she said at last. 'I can't make anything happen. I'm not about to start pulling engine covers off or anything. We'll just hope Travis returns soon and that he can fix it.'

'I could look,' the six-year-old offered.

'I don't think so. This is more complicated than setting a video.' She laughed. It was usually Scott who managed the intricacies of the video recorder. Most kids seemed able to cope with such things when the adults tore out their hair in frustration.

'I've watched Travis. I might be able to see what's wrong.'

Lauren refused the offer and suggested a walk along the lakeside instead. It was typical New Zealand bushland with tall palms and wonderful tree ferns. She pointed things out to the little boy and told him how the warm climate allowed things to grow in the open here.

'Maybe we'd better turn back now. It'll soon be supper time.' They walked back, catching glimpses of the exotic colours of the thermal park across the lake. Columns of steam rose up every few minutes as the pressure underground forced it to the surface. A water-plane landed further up the lake.

'Are they very expensive?' Scott asked. 'I'd be really cool to have one of those, wouldn't it? We could go everywhere really quickly.'

'Forget it, love. They probably cost a fortune and there's no way we could learn to fly it anyhow.'

'Look, Mum. Travis is back.' He rushed towards the house and yelled at the top of his voice. Lauren followed more slowly behind, her heart racing slightly at the mixture of pleasure and relief she was experiencing. Travis was hoisting her son on to his broad shoulders and came towards her.

'Thought you'd gone away for a moment. But then I saw Scotty's fishing pole back there. Knew he wouldn't leave without that. So, how are things?'

'The boat wouldn't start and so we had to go for a walk instead of going across the lake. I wanted to fix it, but Mum didn't think I could.' Lauren couldn't get a word in and shrugged and went to open the door. Her son was certainly completely at ease with the helper.

'I'll put the kettle on,' she muttered as she went through the shop to the kitchen. She smiled happily, feeling secure and much more confident now Travis had come back to them.

'Slow down there, Scotty. Give me a chance to speak to your mum. Has everything been OK? I was worried about you.'

'We've been fine. Nothing much happened.'

'Nothing more from Andrews?'

'Well, yes, actually, I got a letter from him offering five thousand dollars less than before.'

'What did you do with the letter?'

'Threw it into the rubbish bin.'

'We should keep it. Evidence for the future. Have you still got it?'

'Maybe. It'll be a bit messy though.'

She rummaged in the bin and produced a somewhat soggy piece of paper. Travis took it and smoothed it out. He looked troubled but was obviously trying hard not to show it. Lauren busied herself with cooking supper, more enthusiastic now he was back.

'I picked up some good wines when I was in town,' Travis said. 'You want red or white with dinner?'

'You choose. It's chicken.'

'Smells wonderful. I guess red as the white won't be chilled. Oh, and I got something for this young man as well. Here, catch.'

Scott blushed with pleasure as he opened the long thin parcel. 'Oh, wow! Thanks, Travis. Look, Mum, a real fishing rod. It's so cool. Got a reel and everything. Thanks, Travis. Thanks very much.'

'You made a good choice there. It was good of you, but you didn't have to buy anything so expensive.' Lauren felt troubled as the thought of him spending so much when she paid him such a trivial amount of wages. He brushed it aside and went to clean up, ready for the meal.

'You, too, Scott. Go and wash.'

'Can I go fishing after supper?'

'Save it till morning. It'll be dark soon and bedtime soon after supper.

You can catch lunch for tomorrow,' she told him with a grin.

After supper, they sat together, almost like an ordinary family. The adults finished the wine as Scott chatted on.

'What's that?' he asked, spotting one of Travis's bags at the side of the room.

'My computer. I have some work to do so I brought it back with me.'

'Neat,' Scott said, using again his favourite word of the moment. 'Can I play with it?'

'Sorry, but no, Scotty. This is work. No games on it or anything. It's an expensive machine and not to be played with, OK?' The boy turned up his nose and scowled.

'They let us use computers at school. I know how to use it.'

'I mean it. Not to be touched at any time.' Travis looked at him without a smile. The child nodded his agreement and they all saw the message had got through. Lauren was curious.

'What work do you have to do?'

Travis had never mentioned anything he did either past or present. This looked a strange thing for a so-called handyman to own and have to work on. There was something more to him . . . something she knew nothing about.

'All sorts. Business I was involved in before I escaped to your little paradise.' He was saying nothing more and she gave up her questions, for now.

'Bedtime, young man. Go and brush your teeth and get into your pyjamas. I'll come and tuck you in when you're ready.' Grumpily, the child obeyed, obviously reluctant to miss the adults' talk. He knew better than to argue.

'I don't think I'll be too long myself. Had a long drive. Guess we've got a full day tomorrow. There's the boat to fix and we've got to get on with the safety measures. Won't be long till the inspection and it's vital for the future running of the whole enterprise that everything's exactly right. There are plenty of folk out there wanting to take over, besides our Mr Andrews.'

'You seem to have grasped more of the problems than I have,' Lauren said with surprise in her voice. 'And there's the wretched first aid thing looming. Have you heard about the proposed developments in Emerald Valley?'

'I've heard rumours. What's the word around here?'

She repeated Mrs Campion's comments and he nodded. She had confirmed what he suspected.

'It would entirely ruin the peace of this place. Granted the thermals are still there and wouldn't really be affected, except that hundreds more tourists tramping over the land would probably cause endless erosion and then the safety people would insist on many more substantial fences and barriers everywhere. No, we have to fight this. It would totally spoil this whole fragile environment. Excuse me now, I really must go to bed. I'm exhausted and I should make an early start. Thanks for a delicious meal. Night.'

He leapt up and picking up his

laptop, he went into his room. Lauren sat for a few moments, wondering why he had departed with quite such speed. She cleared away the dirty glasses and stacked the dishes. She would tackle them in the morning. Travis came back into the room and took the letter from the windowsill.

'Dried out nicely,' he muttered as he left again. Late into the evening, Lauren heard the sound of him tapping away on the computer. Perhaps he hadn't been quite as tired as he'd made out. However much she wanted him here, clearly, he had a hidden agenda.

5

'Somehow, water had got into the ignition. I really don't understand it. I mean, being a boat, it's actually designed to be near water.' Travis scratched his head with oily fingers. 'Blast,' he said as he realised he'd smeared oil into his hair.

Lauren gave him some kitchen roll and he wiped himself clean again.

'Maybe it got there when it rained. There was quite a storm one night when you were away.'

'Maybe. But it's puzzling. Just an unfortunate incident I s'pose. It's OK. I can fix to easily enough. But we need to know why it happened so it can't happen again.'

Lauren poured coffee for them both and called Scott to come in. Inevitably, he was fishing from the jetty. The new rod had scarcely left his hands since the first thing. Travis had also been out since early morning and he'd concentrated on fixing the ferry boat to make sure it was ready for any passengers. Once it was going again, he planned to continue his efforts to fix the fences and pathways over on the thermal area.

'I've fixed a bell on the shop door,' he told her. 'That way, you can keep the door locked and if any customers come along, they can ring the bell and you can let them in, if they look genuine. If you have any worries, you must phone me right away and I'll come back.'

'Come on, Travis. You're getting paranoid. Surely we can't keep on like this, not through the entire season. If people find everything locked up they'll go elsewhere. How am I supposed to do business like that?'

'Just go along with me for now. It won't be forever. Someone's trying to take away our secret, hidden place and make it into some giant theme park. It has to be worth fighting for doesn't it? Emerald Valley gets it fair share of visitors already. We can't let it all be spoilt by greedy businessmen who don't give a damn, now can we?'

'If you put it like that, I guess. But I can't cope with this top security for long. It's driving me mad and I feel claustrophobic. Cabin fever's setting in.'

'We'll be back for lunch and mean-time, you can get on with your studying. I expect only first class results from you and all in good time for the visitors who'll be arriving before too long. I want this to be the most popular, best kept secret in New Zealand.'

Dutifully, Lauren locked the door after they left and took out her books and papers. She chanted the names of various accidents and their treatments as she did her chores.

When she checked the answers, she had got most of them right and felt her confidence surge. The bell rang and she went into the shop to look through the window. A family were standing out-side, peering in and chatting together.

'Hi. Are you open?' the father asked.

'Sorry. Yes we are. I was just working at the back. Did you want to visit the park? The boat's over the other side. My er . . . my assistant is doing some work over there.' It seemed wrong to call Travis merely her assistant, but she couldn't think of an appropriate title.

'How do we get him to fetch us?'

'There's a bell down on the jetty. Maybe you'd like to ring it?' she said, turning to the children.

They immediately rushed off and clanged the big bell. Within a few minutes, Scott appeared at the top of the steps and he waved, turning back to fetch Travis. 'Won't keep you long. Can I get you anything?'

'Maybe when we get back. You do lunches?'

She nodded, assuming they'd only want rolls or something simple. She would thaw some out while they were away. 'How long do we need for a visit?'

'Couple of hours tops. It's not all that large and you do a lot of climbing. It's a circular route and you end up where you started.'

'You're certainly well hidden here. Gorgeous spot. We'd never have known about it, but for the newspaper article. Thought we'd take a drive out here. S'pose you'll be getting loads of tourists once the season gets going.' The wife was happily chatting on while the children and her husband were out watching the boat arriving.

'What newspaper article was that?'

'An Auckland one. Forget which one it was. Thought we'd come and take a look while it's still unspoilt. They talked about the new development. Shame really. It's such a beautiful peaceful place. Once there's dozens of houses and hotels and all, it will hardly be a secret valley.'

'I haven't seen the article. I know there's been talk locally, but it was just rumour, as far as I know. We all thought so, anyhow. The boat's arrived. I'll catch you later.' Troubled, she took out stuff from the freezer and organised some fillings. They'd always eat up anything that was left over themselves. She glanced at her watch and locking the door, hurried down the road to see Mrs Campion.

'Have you heard anything about some article in the Auckland papers? Saying this whole valley is to be developed? Only we just got some visitors who came because they'd read about it. They'd never heard of the place before.'

'Sorry, love. Haven't heard a thing. But they can't do anything without consultation and if anyone's to be consulted, it has to be us. Maybe I'd better boost my stocks if there's going to be a rush. I'd better get Jamie organised to make a trip into town. Anything you need, dearie?'

'That's kind of you, but I think we're OK for now. I got a bulk order last week. I'd better get back. Family's coming over for some lunch, after their visit. Bye.'

When she saw the boat coming back,

Lauren unlocked the door and was ready waiting to make up the rolls.

'Enjoy the visit?' she asked.

'Quite remarkable,' the man answered. 'It's such a spectacular find in the middle of nowhere. I'm sure that's part of the charm of it all. Won't be the same with all the extra facilities, will it? Though I expect you'll enjoy the extra business.'

'Nothing's definite yet. They've only applied for permission as far as I know. We haven't been notified.'

'I expect the developer was getting in early to get people interested. Well, if you organise a petition against development, you can count me in. Be a tragedy if this idyll was lost.'

'Thanks. I'll bear it in mind.' Before they left, the man handed a card to her.

'You can contact me if you need help. I shall certainly be writing to the correspondence pages to oppose any serious development. Maybe some small additions to the place would help, but we don't want to ruin one of our national treasures, do we? Thanks for a most interesting day.'

When Travis and Scott returned after their day's work, she recounted the news she had gathered. Travis looked grim.

'We've got a bigger fight on our hands than I thought. They're obviously using some contact they have with the media. Quite wrong to be canvassing support at this stage. Leave it with me. I'll see if I can set some wheels in motion.'

After supper, he went to his room and was busy tapping away on his computer. Lauren didn't understand how it could help but he obviously knew what he was doing. She flicked from channel to channel on the television, but there was nothing of interest. She picked up her first aid books and settled down to revise some more.

The next day they had many more visitors and they were all kept busy ferrying them across to the park and preparing the snacks in the café.

They almost ran out of ice-creams and postcards were selling well. Most people had read the article and had come to see the place for themselves, before it was ruined, was the usual comment. They were pleased to have such support.

'Maybe I'm being stupid. Most people would want to improve the takings,' Lauren said that evening. 'I could probably make a fortune, one way or another.'

'But if these plans all go ahead, you won't have a business anyhow. These developers want you out of here so they can use the site and manage the park for themselves.'

'Apart from improving the safety features, nobody can do anything more to the park. It's a trust and I only have the rights to manage it. It's traditionally owned by the Maori and definitely not for sale. Aunt Gwen tried to buy it once and there's legal stuff a mile high in the files. She didn't succeed. So, at least the site itself is safe. This property is certainly all mine, as is the ferry and jetty. Without that, nobody could get to the site.'

'A jetty's nothing. They can build one from any access across the lake. These guys have lawyers on the case and seemingly unlimited funds. Believe me, I know what I'm talking about.'

'I wish I knew what you were talking about. If you know something, you should tell me. You're too mysterious by half. You and that computer of yours. Tapping away till all hours. Are you writing a book or something?'

'It's or something. Not bright enough to write a book. I'd better get to work now. Can I help with clearing up?'

'No. You go and tap whatever it is. I'll do it.'

'The inspection's on Wednesday isn't it? I still have quite a lot to do over there. I'll get over early tomorrow and maybe come back for breakfast later, if that's OK.'

'You're working much too hard, you know. I feel guilty that you get so little pay and get no time off.'

'It'll all be worth it. Besides, it has its compensations. Night.' He dropped a casual kiss on top of her head as he left the room. She frowned after him. What was he really playing at? What was his game?

★　★　★

Wednesday came all too soon. The inspectors arrived, a man and a woman, neither of whom looked old enough to drive, let alone have such responsibility as being inspectors. They had official looking clipboards and reams of forms with tick boxes.

'We'd prefer to make the visit alone,' they told Travis and Lauren. 'Take us over and we'll summon the ferry when we're ready to return. Are there any other visitors over there at the moment?'

'No. None today, as yet.'

'And is there any other way of landing apart from the ferry?'

'No. We have the only concession.'

They were gone for what seemed like hours to the anxious pair waiting on the other side.

'Don't worry,' Travis assured her. 'I checked everywhere last thing yesterday. Every rail's in place. Every warning sign newly painted and firmly fixed. Maybe there're just enjoying the visit.'

'Why are they taking so long?'

Scott dashed in from his lookout position at the side of the jetty.

''Spectors in sight. They're just coming over the top of the hill. Get ready Travis. Can I come across with you?'

'Best not this time. Let's not give them any excuse to find fault. And Pooch better stay behind this time too. You help your Mum get the coffee ready. Make a good impression.'

Lauren watched as he chugged across the lake. It was a beautiful morning and couldn't have made a more pleasant picture for their important visitors. She saw the boat stop and Travis help the grim-faced pair to get out. His face was also missing its usual grin as he shepherded them into the little café.

'You'd like coffee? And can I get you something to eat?' Lauren offered.

'Coffee's fine. We need to sit down with your plans and talk,' the woman said in clipped tones. Travis scowled behind her back and Lauren felt her heart plummeting.

'I'm afraid we can't issue your safety certificate until the damage is repaired. There will be a new inspection next week if you've completed the work and until then, the site must remain closed.'

'I'm sorry? I don't know what you're talking about. Everything was perfectly in order last night.' She glanced at Travis for confirmation. He nodded.

'Well, you know what these places are like. There must have been some sort of eruption. Several posts have been burned and the barrier is no longer adequate. The signs are not clearly placed and in several areas, there could be accidents where visitors could stray off the path and even get badly burned.

And as for you keeping a close tally on the visitor numbers, there were two parties walking around when you clearly said nobody else had gone over today.'

'I don't know how anyone else got over there. As to the damage, I'll get it all fixed right away. I don't know what's been going on over there, but things have clearly been damaged since last night. If it was a fire, then I believe it must have been deliberate. However, that's beside the point.

'If I repair everything immediately, will you come back as soon as possible? It is so important to keep everything moving. We get tourists travelling miles to see this place. It's so bad for our reputation, especially when there's been publicity in the press.' Lauren was fuming inside and desperately trying to keep her temper.

'Even worse, if safety is compromised. Very well. Call us as soon as you are ready and we'll do our best to get back. We shall only need to re-visit the areas we've marked on this map.'

The man ripped several pages off his pad and handed them over. Lauren could see they had duplicated the report and the damaged areas were clearly marked.

'But this is impossible,' Travis exclaimed, peering over her shoulder. 'This was exactly where I replaced all the supports only two days ago.'

'As I said, these parks often have spontaneous fires.'

'You said there were two other parties over there?' The man nodded. 'Are you sure you haven't sold any tickets this morning, Lauren?'

'None at all. You'd have taken them over anyhow. Whoever is there, does not have permission. I assure you, we would know if we'd landed anyone.'

'Is there access from anywhere else?'

'None at all. It's dense scrub behind . . . no tracks or anything. Somebody must have landed the people and then sailed off again.'

'Most unsatisfactory. You can phone

when you've fixed everything and we'll be back as soon as possible. You do need to secure the site though. We can't be responsible for granting your safety certificate and then have just anyone landing whenever they like.'

After they'd left, the three of them sat down to discuss their problems. They speculated about the damage and the unknown visitors.

'Must have been the criminals who did the damage, who were walking round.'

'You're probably right. Maybe I should go and look for them. They must still be there. Anyone seen a boat lately?'

'I don't like you going over there on your own. There must be at least four of them, if two groups were walking round.' Lauren frowned. 'I could see if Jamie would come over with you. There may be some others around too, his friends maybe. And make sure you have your mobile with you.'

'I'll go too. I can hit them with a

hammer or something.'

'No Scott. I need you to stay and look after your mum. You can be lookout from over here and let me know if you see anyone. I'll lend you my binoculars.' Scott was happy with that arrangement.

'I'll call Mrs Campion and see if Jamie's around. I'd be happier if someone went with you.'

She returned, looking grim. 'Seems he's away for a few days with his friends. Some camping trip. Look Travis, you can't go over alone. Maybe we should call the police.'

'I don't somehow think that will help. Tell you what. We'll keep watch from here and if there's any sign of life or boat movements, we shall see and we can be waiting for them. Sometime soon, I will have to drive out to get some more fence materials. I know it would cost more, but metal posts would be better. What do you think?'

'Oh Travis, I really don't know. You think someone's trying to put me out of business, don't you? Something to do with these developers?'

'Maybe. Seems likely. So Scotty, you up for doing some spying?' The child nodded enthusiastically. 'OK then. You and your mum can take turns watching while I go to buy supplies. If you see any movement before I'm back, call the police. And you'd better make a sign to say we're closed until further notice. We can put it out in the road so you don't get folks knocking on the door. Oh, and don't forget to keep the door locked.'

'Where do we keep watch? I thought I'd need to be on the jetty.'

'Maybe you could sit up on the balcony. You'd see clearly from there. Now, no heroics, understand?' Lauren nodded.

'And you take care of yourself,' she told him. 'So you know what you need to buy?'

'Sure. I'll use my credit card and you can pay me back when you're ready.'

'But . . . '

'No buts. It's decided. See you later.'

She watched as he drove away. The clear blue lake shimmered in the sunlight, the lush green vegetation surrounding it. What menace was hidden among the trees and ferns? How could such a glorious place be host to such sinister goings on? Emerald Valley. Place of peace and tranquillity. Maybe it was, once. Would it ever return to that?

With a sigh she went back inside and locked the door. She called up to Scott to see if he was OK and set to work to make the sign. She used a large piece of card and felt pen and then wrapped the whole thing in plastic to keep it dry. There was some wood at the side of the house so she tacked her notice to that and set it up in the middle of the road. Everyone could see it clearly.

The phone rang. It was Mrs Campion. 'You sort out your problems, dearie?' she asked. 'Only Jamie's back now. I can send him down if you like. He's got a couple of mates with him, too.'

'That's kind, but Travis has gone out to get supplies to fix the damage. Whoever was out there on the park has either found a way back or is still there. Scott's keeping lookout. I guess the trouble makers have probably got clean away by now. Thanks anyhow.'

'That's OK, love. Let me know if you need anything. I see you've had to put out a sign. Guess that means you're closed for a bit.'

'Not for long. I'm determined that nobody will close us down. I owe it to Auntie Gwen.'

'Good on ya. See ya soon.'

It seemed a long boring day. Travis returned late in the afternoon, too late to begin work that day. Scott was irritable, once the excitement of possibly seeing the criminals as he called them, had faded and he'd got bored with the whole thing.

They had an early supper and made their plans for the next day. Their main priority was to get the damage put right so they could re-open.

They decided to lock everywhere up, leaving closed signs around, and spend the whole day together, over on the site. Lauren organised a picnic and Travis collected the tools they might need. They all had an early night, ready to get up at dawn and get the work done. That way, they could call the inspectors back and re-open as soon as possible.

★ ★ ★

By the end of the next day, everyone felt exhausted. New metal posts had been rammed in with stout chains across between them.

'Chains will be better than more cross posts, as kids won't be able to climb on them,' Travis had suggested. 'I'll bring the welding gear over tomorrow and we can make sure they are securely fixed.'

'And all the signs are in place again. I think we can safely call the inspectors again tomorrow and by the time they're able to visit, we shall have finished everything.'

'I've been thinking. Maybe I should stay over here for a couple of nights. I can stay in the shelter near the jetty and make sure we don't get unwelcome visitors in the night.'

'No Travis. You can't. It's too dangerous. Nothing is worth taking such a risk. Besides, we need you at home. With us.'

'Oh well, it's worth a thought. And Lauren . . . thanks. It's good to feel needed.'

'For heaven's sake. We certainly do need you. In fact we go as far as to say, we actually like having you around.' She was grinning as she spoke. Like having him around? Understatement of the year.

'Good to know. Lauren . . . I . . . I'm sorry.' He'd put his hand on her arm and seemed to have been drawing her closer but then, something stopped him. What was he afraid of? It seemed that each time he was getting closer, something stopped him and he drew back again.

It was most disconcerting and once more she remembered her resolve not to let him get too close. Some resolve, she thought. In these matters, something far deeper was taking hold. She had no choice in the matter. Travis already meant great deal to her.

6

By some miracle, on the Friday evening, they were in possession of their safety certificate. The inspectors had managed to return and had accepted the new improvements. Travis had also managed to install a camera on the main path leading from the jetty. If anyone passed a beam, it activated the camera and a picture was sent straight back to the house and recorded on their video machine.

'It's very clever,' Scott had announced to the inspectors. 'We get a picture of anyone who walks up the path, even when it's dark. Travis knows about these things,' he said proudly.

'It's certainly a clever idea and should help with the security.' The inspectors seemed quite different on their second visit . . . much more friendly and sympathetic.

'They weren't so bad after all,' Travis remarked.

'They could see how hard we've worked and must have realised we take it all very seriously. Thank you again Travis. I don't know why you're so good to us, but I'm very grateful that you are. I promise, once we're running properly, I'll be able to pay you a better rate.'

'I'm quite happy with things as they are. I'm enjoying the challenge and it's great to spend time in the open air. I think we'll open a bottle of wine to celebrate. What do you say?' She smiled as they went back inside to prepare supper.

It was an extremely busy weekend. Somehow, the word had got round that they were open again. From ten o'clock onwards on the Saturday, a steady stream of visitors came to view the site and Lauren was kept busy serving the customers who came for lunches and souvenirs.

Even Scott was kept busy collecting

tickets and helping Travis cast off the boat and catching ropes when they returned. They had a system of collecting the ticket stubs in a box and each time people returned, the stub was removed. That way, if any stubs were left towards the end of the day, Travis could make a quick trip round the site to find anyone who was still there.

It was during the afternoon that an unfortunate incident occurred. When the ferry came back, Travis came up to the café, carrying a small child, with her parents following behind. The child, a girl of around eight years old, was crying inconsolably.

'Hey, what's happened to you?' Lauren asked.

'She took a tumble down the steps and gashed herself on the leg. Can you do something with it?'

'Let's take a look. Oh you poor thing. That's a nasty cut you've got there. Can I bathe it for you and put on a plaster maybe?'

'All right,' the child agreed. The

parents said nothing. The mother was looking anxious, but the father seemed to be showing little interest.

'Come on then. You can sit on this special chair so I can look at your leg more easily.' She swung the little girl on to a high stool and rolled down the bloody sock.

'You made a good job of this, didn't you?' The child began to wail at the sight of the blood but Lauren gave her a small wrapped sweet to suck and she concentrated on taking the paper off while Lauren got warm water and disinfectant to bathe the wound. Soon, she was satisfied that it was quite clean and she placed a plaster over the length of the cut. 'There. All done.'

She turned to the mother. 'Keep an eye on it for infection and change the dressing daily until it looks as if it is healing. I'm sure it's only a surface scratch and doesn't need stitches.'

'You're very kind. Thank you.' Her husband nudged her hard and pushed her away from the child.

'Are you qualified?' he demanded.

'I'm sorry?' Lauren replied, shaken by his tone.

'Simple enough question. Are you qualified to carry out medical treatment? A nurse. Doctor or something.'

'I'm taking my first aid certificate next week. But this is no more than a cut. Well, a deep scratch really. I'm confident that all is well. It should heal in a few days. Children are so resilient.'

'Let's hope so for your sake. You'll be hearing from me otherwise.' He turned, signalling to the woman to collect the child and stormed out.

'Just a small thank you would have been nice. What was all that about?' Lauren asked.

'Sounds like he was more worried than he let on. You did a good job there. The kid was scared half to death on the way back, but you calmed her beautifully. You'd make an excellent nurse.'

'Thanks ... but I've no such ambitions. It's just mum experience talking here. I've stuck plasters on just about every inch of Scott's legs in my time. Don't know what he meant about us hearing more from him. Is he threatening me, do you think?'

'Forget about it. He's just a worried dad. Now, do you think I've earned a cuppa yet? I'm parched.'

Everything calmed down after the weekend and business was quiet. Travis spent a lot of time in his room tapping away on his computer.

Lauren drove to the local town to stock up the freezer and other stores.

'You can order the souvenir stuff on my computer if you like,' Travis offered. 'Be much quicker.'

'You mean you've got a phone connection for it?'

'Sure have. That's why I've been working up here in my room. I'm able to keep in touch with everything from here. Well, almost everything. I shall have to go away again in a few days, I'm afraid.'

'I see.' She felt her heart plummet

again at the thought of being without his comforting presence. His dark eyes showed concern at her expression.

'Hey, come on. I'm only talking about a few days. Not for a while yet. Just giving you advance warning.'

'OK. I'm sorry, I'm getting too reliant, aren't I? Promise I'll change that. Now, what did you say about placing orders on your infernal machine? Maybe I can do the freezer orders too. And the groceries? Hey, this has possibilities, if I can ever learn how to use it.'

★ ★ ★

'Post's here,' yelled Scott a couple of days later. He came in with an armful of stuff and dumped it on the counter. 'Lots of catalogues. Can I open them?'

Lauren took a quick look and handed several envelopes to her son. There was one heavy envelope with an air of quality about it. She slit it open and gazed at the thick vellum typed page. She went pale and sat heavily on a chair. She heard Scott calling for Travis to come quickly.

'What is it? Andrews again?' He snatched the letter from her trembling fingers as she shook her head.

'Much worse. We're being sued.'

'Good heavens,' Travis almost shouted.

'What's wrong?' Scott asked anxiously.

'The little girl who cut her leg at the weekend. They're claiming compensation. Broken wrist? That's utter piffle. There was nothing wrong with her wrist.'

'There's a copy of a doctor's certificate to say it was broken. She never mentioned her wrist, did she? I mean, all she was complaining about was her leg. I dealt with that. And all this other stuff about compensation and safety issues.'

'It's OK. You've got insurance. That's why getting the safety certificate was so important. The first aid thing is an added extra. Not mandatory at all. You were just helping out, as anyone would if a kid gets hurt. They seemed glad enough at the time. We could have insisted they drove back to wherever they came from and sought medical treatment. That would have cost them money as well. You did it for nothing.'

'But he specifically asked if I was qualified.'

'Yes he did. He's obviously trying to make a few bucks. Some people are like that. Mention compensation and their eyes light up like headlamps. Send it all off to your insurance company and forget it.'

'But what about all that stuff they said about safety and negligence.'

'We've got a brand new safety certificate to wave at them. Ink's barely dry on the page. There are no safety issues and as for the broken wrist, that is definitely not part of this accident.'

However reassuring he was, Lauren couldn't stop worrying about the claim. Maybe the insurance company would investigate the validity of the claim, but the basic facts were correct. She'd treated an injury to a customer and she was unqualified. At least until the following week, with any luck.

'I'll type you a letter to send with all this stuff to the insurance company. I'll just make a copy first, so we have a record of this ... this fantasy of theirs.'

Travis took the papers to his room and a few minutes later, re-appeared with a typed letter and several copies of the documents. Lauren took the letter and read it through. The language was highly professional and very succinct.

'Wow, you've done this before,' she said in admiration. 'It would have taken me days to compose anything that good.'

'Brief and to the point. No need to elaborate. Just need your signature and an envelope. I assume the insurance premiums are paid up to date?'

'Yes. Gwen paid them for the year in advance. I just hope this does the trick.'

* * *

It was an anxious few days, not helped by yet more vandalism at the site across the lake. The hidden cameras showed nothing. Someone had obviously found a way to get over to the park and commit their nasty little crimes.

'I reckon we're going to need several cameras. If we cover the areas we can't see from here, which granted, is most of it, we might catch the culprits on film. That way we shall at least know who's trying to damage our business.'

'That'll cost a fortune though,' Lauren protested.

'I know a supplier. He'll let us have a system cheap. Don't worry about it. I'll organise it all.'

The conversation was interrupted by a phone call. Lauren's face went ashen as she listened.

'But this is ridiculous. I only washed the kid's leg and stuck a plaster on. No . . . I know I don't have qualifications but neither do most mothers. I was only trying to comfort the poor kid. No . . . I didn't say that . . . I never said it.' Travis went over to her and put a comforting hand on her shoulder. He felt her trembling and could see she was angry.

'Very well. But please don't expect me to renew with your company next year. This is exactly the sort of thing that I pay your extortionate premiums to cover.' She slammed the phone down and burst into tears.

'I gather the insurance company don't want to know about the claim?' Travis asked.

'I'm not qualified to show sympathy or stick plasters on bleeding legs. Evidently I should have insisted they went to a hospital or a doctor and got proper treatment. Don't think I'll even bother to take this first aid exam. What's the point?'

'Of course you'll take it. This is precisely why you'll take it. If you had got the qualification, they'd have no case. Yes, I know.' He held his hand up and she began to protest. 'You'd probably have done exactly the same thing next week after the exam as you did before. It's the wonderful glory of official bits of paper. Produce a certificate and the world is happy.'

'Meantime, the company is refusing to meet their claim and either it goes to court or I pay up and keep quiet about it. Either way, it's money I don't have. I don't see why I should pay masses of compensation anyway or legal fees for some lawyer to argue the case. It clearly wasn't my responsibility. Heavens, we even have signs saying we're not responsible for injuries.'

'Disclaimer notices can still be challenged,' Travis said thoughtfully. 'The trouble is, even if you pay out for their claim it doesn't guarantee you won't be charged with negligence. I know it's grossly unfair, but they could still bring a case. Bad publicity at the very least.'

★　★　★

Lauren slept little that night. She barely remembered the sense of excitement she had been feeling when the business was left to her and the future possibilities stretched before her.

Now it all seemed like a nightmare with an uncertain future. Maybe she should accept the odious Mr Andrews' offer and take what she could get. There might be enough for her and Scott to make a new start. She sat up in the darkness and sent an apology to her aunt.

'I'm sorry, Auntie Gwen. I've let you down so badly . . . after all the years you worked hard to build up the business and now it's all going pear-shaped. What would you have done?'

Lauren lay down again and tried in vain to sleep. When the first glimmer of light showed through the curtains, she got up and made some tea, hugging the mug to warm her icy hands.

'Hey, what are you doing up so early?' Travis asked, laying a hand on her shoulder. It felt wonderfully comforting. She missed the warmth of another human's contact . . . it seemed so long since Adam had been there for her. 'I guess you were fretting and not able to sleep. This tea fresh?'

He moved the comforting hand from her shoulder and she felt a cold space where it had been. What she really needed was a soothing hug, but that would be far too risky with Travis. Besides, she wouldn't be able to face the possibility of rejection if he drew away. She poured some tea and tried to busy herself with breakfast preparations.

The post arrived with another letter from Andrews, offering a further reduction of eight thousand dollars. 'At this rate, I'll be giving it to him,' she said miserably.

'That's just what he wants you to think. I just know he's behind all the trouble and it wouldn't surprise me to learn that even this accident and the compensation case with the child, is something to do with him.'

'Oh surely not. Nobody would deliberately hurt a child and try to make a claim from it. No, I can't believe anyone would be that evil. What you're suggesting is paranoid in the extreme.'

'I'm not suggesting it was a deliberate act. But maybe the family are employed by him and he's capitalising on the accident. A lucky break for him, pardon the pun.'

'Poor little kid. I won't believe she was part of it.'

'No. But suppose the family were sent here to spy out the land. See exactly what's going on . . . especially if he's also organising the sabotage. Her accident was fortuitous maybe, but I still think he's behind the claim. If he can ruin your business he'll be able to buy it for next to nothing.

'No, he's definitely got someone on the ground here. Someone local who knows the set-up. I'm going to stay over there on the site for a night or two. I have to see what's going on and how they're landing there. I'll take Pooch with me. He'll alert me if there's someone around. You'll be safe enough here. We've both got mobile phones.'

'I don't like it at all. Don't you think I should just give up? Take what's on offer and try to start again somewhere?'

'We can't let that happen. We can't let greedy folk into this valley and allow them to destroy it all.'

'I know you're right, but I'm very frightened. What would I do without you? You're never going to settle forever for a life in this remote place. You're obviously cultured . . . you read a lot, like good music. What are you doing with your life? You're working as a poorly-paid general handyman, employed by a woman who is probably about to go bankrupt. That's hardly a bright future, is it?'

'I have my reasons. I love it here and the woman you're talking about is a very special lady. She's brave and an excellent mum to her little boy.' Lauren felt her cheeks burning. Her heart was racing and she was totally lost for words. She stepped towards him, willing to risk everything for the hug she so desperately needed.

He touched her arm, slowing her down. 'Not now love. Not yet.' He turned away and opened the door. 'Lovely morning.'

Lauren felt sick. It was a clear rejection. But his words simply contradicted his actions. He sounded as though he believed they had something special between them, but when she responded, he withdrew. She felt confused and foolish. She was also worried by his plan. She feared for his safety as well her own and Scott's.

'I'll just take a sleeping bag and a flask of coffee,' Travis decided. 'And maybe a roll or two. I'll be back for breakfast. I'll take the little dinghy rather than the ferry boat and then I can hide it. If anyone does come over, they'll be unaware of anything. If I go at dusk, I shouldn't be seen.'

'I'm really not happy at all,' Lauren protested. 'It's too dangerous.'

'I'll be fine. Now you make sure

everywhere is locked up and secure. And keep your phone by you at all times.'

Silently, he rowed across the lake. It was almost dark and the sounds of night creatures filled the air. Squeaks and plops and the sounds of birds broke the silence.

Lauren went inside and locked the doors, staring out of the window to watch him land. He was practically invisible, apart from a quick flash of torchlight as he stowed the boat in the reeds.

Scott was safely in bed and the house was silent. Too silent. She put some music on and tried to concentrate on her first aid papers. Eventually, she gave up and went to bed early. She peered out of the window across the lake to see if she could see anything, but it was all dark. She thought of calling Travis on his phone, but decided against it, as the ringing might alert anyone else who could be on the site.

It was a tense night and every creak

of the house sounded like thunder. Eventually, she drifted into a light sleep and was awoken sometime later by a loud crash of breaking glass. She got up quickly and grabbed her phone and old walking stick belonging to her late aunt.

Bleary eyed, Scott stumbled out of his room. She silenced him, motioning him to get behind her. They crept along to the kitchen and pushed the door open, switching on the light at the same time. A furry face peered out of big eyes, blinking in the light. It was a possum, standing surrounded by broken glass.

'Wow, he's just a bit cute,' Scott called out.

'Don't touch him. Just open the door and we'll try to scoot him out.' Scott did as he was told and the creature padded off into the darkness.

'I don't see how it could have broken the window. The animal isn't that large and the force it would have taken to break the glass . . . well. I don't believe it. I'm going to call Travis. I want him back here. I reckon this was someone trying to break in. The possum must have got in by pure chance.'

'But they can climb really well. My teacher said so at school. Maybe it did get in by itself,' Scott said. But Lauren was already pressing the key pad on the phone. Instantly, Travis answered.

'What's up? I thought I heard something like breaking glass, from over here. Sound travels over water particularly well at night. Are you all right? And Scott?'

'There was a possum in the kitchen, but I don't think it could have broken that window and climbed in all by himself. Are you OK? Did I wake you?'

'I wasn't asleep. I've been up and down all night. Kept hearing things, but I can't see anything. Expect it's the ground making it's own peculiar noises. All the thermal activity that goes on over here, it sounds a bit like massive indigestion, deep underneath it all. Do you want me to come back over?'

'Yes please. I'm really feeling shaken, even though nothing much has happened. The broken window's also wide open if anyone else came along . . . '

7

'I'm still certain that our Mr Andrews is somehow behind all this,' Travis announced after he had replaced the glass in the window. I've bought some wire to put over the windows so it can't happen again. I know it seems extreme, but until things have been sorted out, we need to take every precaution. I've also ordered an alarm system for the house. It should arrive tomorrow.'

'How much is all this costing?' Lauren asked anxiously. 'Only you know the situation at the moment. I'm down to rock bottom with the bank and with this case hanging over us . . . '

'Don't worry about anything. I'll give you the bill when you're up and running properly.'

'Why are you so good to us?'

'Let's just say I think I may have

found somewhere I'd like to be. I want to make sure it stays somewhere exactly as it is right now.'

For a few days things seemed to be stable. There were odd incidents and one day, the power was off for several hours, but it was fixed and they put it down to coincidence rather than any deliberate tampering. Lauren even managed to go to town to take her first aid certificate and despite all her other worries, she passed with flying colours.

'We shall frame the certificate and put it on the wall where everyone can see it. Everyone should know that you are fully competent to treat minor injuries,' Travis told her. 'Well done, Lauren. I'm proud of you.' He kissed her cheek and she found herself blushing with pleasure.

The pleasure didn't last for long. In the mail were two further letters from Andrews, posted morning and evening of the same date. Each contained an offer for her property, each lower than the previous ones.

'Shame I can't sue him for harassment,' Lauren said.

'If we could only prove he was behind the problems and vandalism, maybe we could. Trouble is, the police have nothing to go on and some of the incidents are trivial and inconvenient rather than serious criminal damage. Look, Lauren, I know this is bad timing, but I do have to go away again. Only a few days but something I really have to do. I'm sorry, but I can't avoid it.'

'I see.' Lauren was tight-lipped and looked worried. 'If you must, you must. Your timing is indeed, terrible. But no doubt I'll cope. I usually do.'

'You can certainly call the police if you need to. You could even go away yourself for a few days. Shut everything up and take a break. It would do you good. Why not?'

'Perhaps it would, but I don't exactly have money to waste on a holiday. We'll manage somehow. And yes, I can always call the police if I need them.'

After he left, both she and Scott felt

quite bereft. The child was grumpy and nothing she could do made him feel any better. He was missing his idol. A few tourists were coming down and by the end of the day, she felt worked off her feet, ferrying them over and trying to keep the shop and café open. She was just about to close the day after Travis had left when a young couple arrived. They were well dressed and drove a newish car.

'I understand you do bed and breakfast?' the young man asked. 'The lady down the road sent us. The lady at the store?'

'Oh, Mrs Campion. Well, normally, I can take guests but it's a little difficult at the moment.'

'Oh, dear. We've had such a long drive and we can't face going on to Rotorua. We so much want to see the thermal site and it's a bit late tonight. We won't be any trouble.'

Lauren looked at them uneasily. They looked nice and seemed genuine. Besides, it would be good to have someone in the house with Travis away.

'Well, OK then. I can't offer much in the way of dinner. I wasn't expecting visitors. But there's basic stuff in the freezer and it won't take long to sort the room. If you'd like to fill in the registration card, I can make you some tea to be going on with.'

'That's really great. Thanks very much. Wonderful site you've got here.'

She busied herself with clean sheets and took out some fish from the freezer. The young couple went for a walk while she prepared the meal. Scott was chattering to them outside when they returned and she felt comfortable. Even Pooch seemed to approve of the guests. All the same, she felt Travis should know and she dialled his number. There was no reply and she could not even leave a message. Very strange.

★   ★   ★

The next morning, the visitors were up early. Lauren provided breakfast and asked about their plans for the day.

'We'll go and visit this remarkable looking site after we finish breakfast, if that's OK. Then we'll push on before lunch. Thanks for everything. You've really made us welcome and we appreciate it. We'll collect our stuff after the visit.'

Lauren took them across, showing them the bell they must ring when they'd finished their visit. She insisted on Scott accompanying then, despite his wish to stay and fish. Several other tourists arrived and Scott carefully stowed the ticket stubs in the container they used to keep a tally on the numbers.

Lauren was busy making snacks when their bed and breakfast guests were packing their car to leave. To her horror, they got in and drove away before they had paid their bill. She rushed outside but they had got clean away and were driving away up the hill.

'Oh, no, I don't believe it. They seemed so nice,' she said angrily to

Scott. The other customers looked concerned.

'You should get some help, love. Can't expect to do everything yourself,' one of them suggested.

'My help's having a holiday,' she said sourly. She wondered if Jamie, Mrs Campion's son, could be spared just for a few days. She planned to phone and ask later if she ever got a moment again.

When the day was finally over, she sank into an exhausted heap on the sofa. She tried to dial Travis and once more, failed to catch him.

'Do you think he's left us forever and ever?' Scott asked miserably. 'Only he never said goodbye properly, did he? And he's left some of his stuff behind.'

'I'm sure he'll be back. It's a case of when. Don't worry about it.' But she could see the child was very upset. Once more she tried to tell herself that they shouldn't rely on him so much. One day, he might well return to whatever life he'd left behind.

The next morning brought an even greater shock. The letter arrived giving the time of the case for the compensation claim. It was only a few days away and she knew she had to contact Travis quickly.

Time and again she tried his number but it was always unavailable. She consulted the solicitor that Travis had organised and though he tried to support her, he was also giving a most worrying message.

'Just in case things don't work out, you should be prepared to, well, to stay. Have you got someone to look after your little boy?'

'Not at the moment, no. My assistant is away and I don't seem able to contact him. I'll just have to hope he'll be back in time. You don't seriously think I'll go to jail, do you? I mean to say, there isn't really a case to answer.'

'No, of course not. You'll probably get away with a fine if they do find against us.'

As she finally put the phone down, Lauren was beginning to feel positively ill. How could this nightmare be happening to her? All she wanted was a peaceful life, with good honest hard work to make a future for herself and Scott. Coming to New Zealand was clearly the worst thing she had ever done.

Where could Travis be when she needed him so badly? His timing couldn't have been worse. How necessary was his trip, really and truly? She even wondered if he'd somehow known this could happen.

A thought struck her. Maybe he was associated with Andrews in some way. He seemed to know more about the man than he was ever willing to let on.

Several long days dragged by with nothing, not even a message from Travis. The dreaded day arrived for the hearing. She had arranged to take Scott to Mrs Campion's for the day, praying that she would be able to collect him that evening.

It was a small, informal looking courtroom used for preliminary hearings in local cases. She was directed to a small waiting room and she sat dreading the possibility of seeing the man and his wife who were bringing the claim. She was near to tears and glad that nobody else was in the room to see her. At last, her solicitor came in.

'Oh, Mrs Wilmshaw, I'm so sorry to keep you waiting. I tried to call you at home, but you'd already left. Then I was in court with another client. However, to business. It seems the claim has been withdrawn. The claimants decided not to pursue the case, so we've been told. No reason given. But I expect you're very relieved. I have to say it wasn't looking too hopeful. These cases are always difficult, especially when a child is involved. Still, all's well that ends well, eh? There'll just be my bill to settle and you're free to go.'

Lauren felt the tears filling her eyes

again. Her emotions were running at fever pitch it seemed and she almost hugged the man, except he wasn't a huggable type. He handed her an envelope. She slit it open and took out his bill. She gasped at the size of it and wished she could earn such a sum so easily.

'Oh, dear, I didn't bring a cheque book. Under the circumstances I hadn't realised I'd need it. May I post it to you?'

'Of course, madam. I always like to be prepared and these things can drag on if you let them. I'll expect settlement within a day or two?'

'Sure. Thanks,' she murmured politely. Somehow he was not a man who would inspire confidence in anyone and she hoped she would never have to see him again. Though she felt highly relieved and delighted to be going home, she was highly irritated at the waste of time.

She was also very distressed at being put through such anxiety and all so needlessly. She was still puzzled as to the reasons behind the case. Why on earth would they drop it so suddenly, unless they knew it would fail or if someone had paid them off.

Travis? Maybe he was behind it. He certainly gave the impression that he had money to spare.

'Mum, you're home early,' Scott called out as she stopped the car. 'I've had a really great time. Mrs Campion let me help make up orders for the chalets. You get a list and then have to find everything on the list and put it in the boxes and then tick each thing off on the list. Then you . . .'

'OK, Scott, I get the picture. Hi, Mrs C. It all turned out OK. They withdrew the complaint. I can't tell you how relieved I feel.'

'That's terrific. So now it's everything back to normal and you can get on with your life.' She rushed over to Lauren and gave her a hug. 'This is such a relief. Such good news.'

'Hopefully. A few problems still to sort, but nothing quite as bad as that particular one.'

'And when's Travis coming back?'

'I don't know. I still haven't heard from him.'

Everything at home looked exactly as she had left it and it all seemed like a very long time ago since early that morning. Pooch gave them both a huge welcome. He'd been left in the house and should she have failed to return, Mrs Campion was going to let him out and look after him.

Once more, she tried to call Travis, though she was without hope, expecting the phone to ring out. To her surprise, he answered. She told him the good news and he sounded genuinely delighted.

'I was going to call you. I'll be back first thing tomorrow,' he told her. 'Have the coffee on and I shall probably need a very large bacon roll. Or even two.'

She laughed and felt her heart sing. She pushed away the unwelcome doubts she'd felt and knew that things were going to work out. For once, she slept well and woke slightly later than normal. She pulled the curtains back and saw Travis's van pulling up outside. She flung her robe on and rushed down to open the door.

'Good to see you,' he said, putting his arms round her in a big hug. Scott came down to join them and Lauren closed her eyes, savouring the moment. 'So, why don't I smell coffee? And bacon? Don't tell me I'm here before you're up and running?'

'You certainly are.' She made breakfast and caught up on the news. They talked of the compensation case and he expressed relief that it had all worked out. 'I still don't understand how they could drop it after all the fuss they made.'

'No knowing with some folks. Maybe they got cold feet.'

'He didn't strike me as a cold feet type. You're sure you didn't have anything to do with it?'

'Me? I don't know what you mean.'

'Are you sure you didn't pay them off?'

'Now, Lauren. Would I allow anyone

to get away with something like that? Now, let's move on. Are we open for business or what? And where's my brekkie?'

They fell into an easy routine over the next few days. There were a few visitors, but nothing too strenuous and they managed easily. They were beginning to believe that the worst was over when another blow was struck. Despite the increased safety measures, they discovered the landing stage had been badly damaged one morning.

There were gaping holes in the decking and the handrails were very loose. It was clearly deliberate sabotage. Nothing like that could have happened by accident.

'I don't understand how it could have happened,' Travis moaned. They must have used hefty equipment to cause this much damage. Why didn't we hear anything? And we put cameras overlooking the whole thing and nobody could have seen where they were hidden. Even so, someone's smashed them to pieces. It'll take hours to repair all this. And it's all the heaviest timber. The most expensive sort.'

'All we need now is for another of Mr Andrews' offers to arrive. If it does, surely it's proof of his involvement, wouldn't you say?'

'Looks that way,' Travis agreed.

'Shouldn't we notify the police? We can't simply go on fixing every bit of vandalism when it happens. My bank account can't take it for one thing. Besides, if the police are involved then surely it's a legitimate insurance claim.'

'I'll get the wood and fix up the landing stage,' Travis said wearily. 'We can't take anyone over till it's done. As for the police, I don't know if it's even worth it. Please yourself. You know what the insurance company was like last time you tried to claim. It also means the premiums would be totally unaffordable next year.'

The phone rang. Lauren answered it and Travis watched her face as she tried to answer the call. She was very angry indeed.

'Can you tell me who gave you this information? I see. Well, I can assure you it will be fixed within the next twenty-four hours. If you think it necessary. Yes, of course.' She plonked the phone down. 'Can you believe it? That was the safety people. Wanted me to confirm that the landing stage is damaged and what are we doing about it. Say it was an anonymous caller who told them. And they'll need to inspect it again before we can use it. Honestly. This is no joke any more. It's all out war.'

'I doubt we can get that lot fixed within twenty-four hours. Materials will have to be ordered and delivered.'

When the post arrived there was an even more ludicrous offer for the property. 'This is ridiculous,' Travis said as he stormed out. 'I'm going to patrol the site all night if necessary. They're not getting away with it.'

True to his word, Travis seemed to

exist with scarcely any sleep for the next few nights. He made a camp in the bushes over in the park and every hour, walked around the site. He did it during most of the night. How long could he keep this up? The stress was becoming unbearable.

'I seriously think I ought to give in and sell the property,' she told him one evening. 'You're exhausting yourself and it's all for nothing. This wretched man is determined to win just as he warned me. And he obviously has the resources to do exactly what he wants to intimidate us. I'm paying you next to nothing as it is and I know I simply can't manage the place alone. I proved that well and truly.'

She had never forgiven herself for allowing her guests to leave without paying. She'd written to the address they'd given, but the letter had been returned as the place was non-existent. If she hadn't been so busy she would have organised the whole thing better.

'You mustn't give in. Let's have one

more shot at fighting this. I'm sure I'm near the answer. Please, Lauren, give us a bit longer. I'm fine, honestly. Don't need much sleep anyway.'

'I'll think about it.' He went to his room and shut the door. She heard him tapping away on his computer once more and she left him to it.

'I'm going to try and sort out the latest damage,' Travis called as he left the house.

'OK, thanks. I'm going to do some washing. Have you got any dirty clothes?'

'Couple of shirts, if you don't mind. They're on the chair in my room.'

She went into his room to collect them and peered out of the window to watch him crossing the lake. Pooch was perched high in the bows in his favourite place and Scott was holding the tiller, carefully supervised by Travis. It was a pleasant sight despite all the traumas surrounding them. It would be such a shame for Scott to have to lose all this if they returned to a city lifestyle.

As she turned back, she noticed that Travis's computer was still switched on. She stared at it, wondering what would happen if she turned it off. She was totally ignorant about computers, but she did at least know that you had to do something special to them before you switched them off. She frowned. Better not, she told herself. I might break it.

She was turning away when the words caught her eye. *Leyton Financial Services*. Leyton rang a bell but she couldn't think why for a moment. Leyton. Travis's name was Leyton but everyone called him Travis, she remembered. She'd never thought about it again.

She looked down the page. It was a list of names and presumably, their account numbers. One name jumped off the screen. *Charles Andrews Development and Acquisitions*. She went cold. She sat heavily on the bed. His bed. He was in cahoots with Charles Andrews after all.

Everything he'd said to her, all he'd

done to help was with a purpose. He wanted to enhance the business to make it an even better bargain when she sold to him.

How could he? Why had he done this to her and Scott. Scott. She realised her precious son was over on the other site with that traitor. He wanted to buy the whole enterprise at rock bottom prices. What a gullible idiot she had been. Why, she hadn't even seen his references. No wonder!

8

Anxiously, she watched and waited for them to return. She hadn't quite made up her mind what to say to Travis. The evidence was undeniable. It was quite clear that Andrews was a client of Travis's business and that they were working together in some way. She laughed ironically to herself. She'd known that he was obviously much more than a handyman. He was a sophisticated man who it seemed, ran a business empire of some sort.

No wonder he was willing and able to lend her money to fix the fences. He was probably richer than anyone else she knew. He'd made a complete and utter fool of her. He had to go.

She paced up and down, wondering if she should challenge him with the truth she'd discovered or should she wait for him to come clean? She didn't believe for one moment that he would harm her or Scott.

'There's heaps to do, Mum,' Scott informed her. 'We've got to go and buy wood . . . timber, it's called . . . for the job and lots of big nails. Travis says I can go with him this afternoon. Is that OK?'

'Well, I really could do with some help here. If we get visitors, I need you to help with the tickets.'

'But nobody can go to the site. You'll have to put up the closed sign again.'

Lauren frowned. She didn't want her son to go off with this man that she could no longer trust. All the same, she didn't want to arouse his suspicions.

'Well, all right then, if Travis is OK with it.'

'Sure. Fine by me.' He went to his room and obviously had switched off the computer. He made no comment about it and she hoped he assumed she hadn't noticed it.

He and Scott drove off soon after lunch and she was once more left with her thoughts. She was working on a plan. One which would bring the two men face to face and she would then, surely know if they were in collusion. If it didn't work, she could fall flat on her face but the uncertainty of not knowing was driving her crazy.

Whatever the situation really was, she knew that she cared a great deal for Travis. She hoped her instincts were still right, even though the evidence against him was looking pretty damning.

With her closed sign out in the road, she was left alone for the afternoon. She busied herself cooking various cakes and cookies she could put out in the café at some point, if she was ever able to run it again. She stowed them in the freezer and set to work on making a special supper. She would tell Travis of her intentions over the meal and wait for his reaction.

'We're back,' yelled Scott, bursting in through the front door. 'It was really neat at the timber yard. Massive piles of wood ... timber ... some of them huge and like proper trees. We've had to order the timber cos it was too big to put in the van. But we got nails. Lots of them.'

'Good. Sounds like a useful after noon. Could you give Pooch a bit of a run? He's been inside with me.'

'Sure. What's for supper? I'm starving.'

'Steak pie. It's not ready yet so off you go for a while.'

'Come on, Pooch,' he yelled, tearing off at his usual top speed.

Travis came in and she gave him a cup of tea. 'Thanks. My, something smells good. I hope that's supper.'

'Certainly is. Another hour though. I wasn't sure when you'd be back so I didn't put it in the oven.'

'Smells like a bottle of red would be appropriate to go with that. I've still got a few bottles left in my room. My private wine cellar. Sound like some sort of secret drinker, don't I? But I do enjoy a decent bottle of wine.'

'Sounds good to me. I'd better get on

with the veggies.' She hoped she sounded casual and that the shaking she felt inside was well hidden. She was fine until he came to stand behind her. He put his hands on her shoulders.

She felt a shiver run down her spine and her insides turned to jelly. Somehow, she kept herself under control and turned to smile at him. His dark brown eyes seemed to look right inside her, as if he could read what she was thinking.

'I know you're worried. It'll be all right. I promise you. We'll work through all this.'

However much Lauren had been longing for him to kiss her, she knew this was not right, especially not now. As he'd once said to her, this is not the time. She hoped he couldn't hear her heart pounding. Besides, aware of her recent suspicions, she dare not let herself get involved any deeper.

'If I don't get some potatoes in a pot, supper will be late. Are you going to shower? If so, you could just about fit it in now.'

'Do I smell or something?' he asked anxiously.

'Course not,' she laughed. 'Only you usually take a shower before supper. I just thought . . . well . . . you know.' He smiled at her.

'You're looking distinctly flustered. I was only teasing. I do always have a shower before supper so yes, I'll go and do it right away.'

Red-faced, Lauren concentrated on the vegetables, hoping he wasn't suspicious. If only he didn't have the effect of turning her very bones to a quivering mass of jelly when he was near, it might be a bit easier. Why did she have to go and fall in love with someone so unsuitable? Someone who might well be trying to cheat her out of her inheritance.

'This is great,' Scott said stuffing his third helping of pie into his mouth. 'I'm starving.'

'You can't possibly be starving after all you've eaten. And to think, I was once worried that you didn't eat enough to keep a gnat alive.'

'That was before Travis came. I'm going to grow tall and strong like him. Good pie isn't it, Travis?'

'Certainly is,' Travis agreed. 'Even my mother's pie was never this good.'

'You've never talked about your parents,' Lauren said, realising this was the first time he'd even mentioned either of his parents. 'Are they still alive?'

'No. Both dead. Mum died a couple of years ago. Just after Dad.'

'I'm sorry. You must miss them.'

'Mum's mum and dad are both dead as well. It's a shame people have to die. I don't know why they do,' Scott said matter-of-factly. Travis and Lauren said nothing. What was there to say?

'So, where did your parents live?' she asked.

'One of the islands off Auckland. Rather isolated, but they loved it.'

'And what was your father's occupation?'

'You know, I'm absolutely full to

bursting,' Travis commented, clearly avoiding her questions. 'Hope you haven't made a big dessert.'

'There's ice-cream, ice-cream or ice-cream,' she suggested.

'I'll have ice-cream,' Scott said. 'Would have done anyhow, even if you'd said anything else.'

He trotted off to the freezer.

'I need to talk after supper, if that's OK. If you have time.' Lauren tried to smile as she spoke, but her lips wouldn't function properly.

'You sound serious. Something wrong? Something more than usual?'

'After Scott's in bed.' He came back into the room carrying a large tub of ice-cream. 'Find it all right?'

'Course. We're having this one. Honey . . . something. Can't read it. It's good having a sort of shop. You get to choose all sorts of things like ice-cream flavours. I'm glad we came here.'

Lauren smiled weakly and reached for some glass bowls.

'So you see,' she said some time later,

'I don't really have much choice. If I don't sell up, I shall be bankrupt anyway. I can't believe Andrews will seriously pay so little money. If he really knows I'm willing to sell, he has to up his offer. That way, I shall be able to afford somewhere for us to live and I can always get a job to keep us.'

'But Lauren, after all we've been through. You can't seriously mean it? And I doubt very much that he'll give you even as much as his last offer, for the business. If you contact him, he'll know he's won and that he has you over a barrel.'

'But I can't go on fighting. It's too stressful and it's not fair to Scott. No, I'm determined to call him tomorrow. But I do intend to name my price. If he wants this place badly enough, he'll pay for it. He's got to.'

'You've simply got no idea of who or what you're dealing with. He's obviously totally unscrupulous and what's more, he doesn't care who he hurts in the process.'

'Sounds as though you might know him?'

Travis looked uncomfortable for a moment.

'I know his type. You don't want to do business with people like him. Believe me. It will end in grief.'

'If you don't like it, you can always find yourself another job. One which will actually pay you a living wage.'

His jaw tightened and he looked grim.

'I like this job. But, if you're firing me . . . what choice do I have?'

'I'm not firing you. Not yet anyhow. But once I've sold the business, you'll have to find something else. Meanwhile, you can stay on if you want to.' The words nearly choked her and at any moment she felt as if she might break down and cry. She bit her lip hard in an attempt to control herself.

'Lauren, you're making this so difficult for me. I don't want to leave you and Scott. Not at all. But this man . . . this Andrew is a scoundrel. Yes, I do

141

know of him. He will undoubtedly ruin this valley with a mass of so called attractions and buildings everywhere. Glitzy entertainment for the masses. The natural beauty of the place will be lost forever.'

'They wouldn't allow him to do that would they? But, I'm not happy either. You must realise, there's nothing else I can do.'

* * *

She lay awake much of the night. Travis had made a good case and still given nothing away. Angrily, he'd gone off somewhere round the back of the building to work, saying little.

All the same, she felt she had to carry out her plan and right after breakfast, she made a call. She spoke to the secretary, who was certain Mr Andrews would be in touch as soon as possible, but that he was not available at this time.

Feeling a sense of anticlimax, she put

the phone down. She'd expected at least to speak to him. Not wanting to be far away from the phone, she busied herself with tidying and cleaning areas that didn't really need it. But there was no call, nothing. Later in the morning, Scott came running in excitedly.

'Mum, there's one of those water plane things landing and it's coming right up to our landing stage. It's really brill. Do you think I might get to go in it?'

This was it. Rather than a simple phone call, the man had obviously decided to visit in person. She might have guessed he'd have his own exotic method of transport readily available.

'Certainly not. Now just keep out of the way. I've got some important business to sort out. You can tell Travis what's going on. He may want to be on hand.' She tugged off her apron and straightened her hair.

'Mrs Wilmshaw. I'm pleased to hear you're ready to sell to me. I have the documents all ready for you to sign. You won't regret your decision.'

'Do come in,' she said somewhat belatedly, as he was already inside the café. 'Can I get you some coffee?'

'I don't think so,' he said with an expression that suggested he wouldn't deign to drink anything in this place. He handed her a sheaf of papers. She glanced down at the pages, looking for the price he was offering. 'Down at the bottom, right next to the place you need to sign.' He could see exactly what she was looking for.

'But this is . . . this is ludicrous. It's less than half what you offered in the first place. That's my price. Your first offer and you're getting a bargain at that.'

'My dear good woman. I said at the time that it was a one-off offer. That the price would go down each time you refused. You knew that.' His smooth face looked bland and uncompromising. Oily, even. His eyes were pale blue and icy cold. There wasn't a shred of good humour to be seen.

'That's not legal. I'm sure it's not. In any case, you know what you can do with your pathetic offer. I'm not interested.'

'I shall only be offering half of this amount by the end of the week,' he said with his sickening smile fixed to his nasty face. 'You'll be begging me to take if off your hands next week. Just you wait and see.'

'That sounds very much like a threat to me. You've been harassing me for weeks. I suspect you're behind all the vandalism and all the other difficulties we've encountered. Water in the boat's ignition. Compensation claims? Does that wretched man work for you as well? And the guests who left without paying? I bet they're all something to do with you.'

'Such paranoia. You'll be blaming me for the bad weather too, soon. All your word against mine. No witnesses. I doubt you'd get anywhere with your foolish accusations. Last chance to take my offer? Can you seriously afford to wait?' His silky voice was even more irritating than his words and she lost her temper completely.

'Get off my property,' she snapped.

'Very well. I'll look forward to hearing from you early next week.'

'You don't scare me. Just go.' She was clenching her fists and almost biting her tongue to keep herself from saying things she might regret.

'I'll give your little boy a ride in my plane if you like. He's very keen.'

'Don't you lay a finger on my son. I'll call the police if you as much as speak to him. Now, get out of my sight.'

Slowly Mr Andrews, developer, walked away from the building. He glanced around as he did so, peering under the house and kicking at the wooden supports around the landing stage.

She had the thought that he was looking to see what could most easily be removed to cause the most damage. She gave a shiver and went to where Scott and Travis had been hiding.

'Oh, there you are. I wondered what

was going on. I could have done with your support. Odious man.'

'I take it the meeting didn't go as planned? Sorry. I kept out of the way on purpose. I thought you wanted to handle it on your own.'

'Well, I tried. But he wouldn't even match the offer he made last week. He threatened me again. Even hinted that he might take Scott off somewhere. Said I'd be begging him to take the property off my hands by the end of the week.'

'I warned you. He's a out-and-out scoundrel. An obnoxious character altogether.'

Angrily, Travis turned quickly and ran towards the man, just as he was about to board his aircraft.

Andrews stopped when he saw him approaching. He hesitated, looking momentarily anxious and then his eyes narrowed. He signalled to the pilot to start up and climbed back into his aircraft.

Travis got to the end of the landing

stage just as the plane taxied away over the water. He shook a fist at the plane and turned back to Lauren and Scott. She looked away. It was interesting.

Obviously the two men knew each other. Despite Travis's expression of anger, clearly, Andrews had been very surprised to see him. Was it really because they were working together?

'I'm going after him. I think I know where he might be heading with his aircraft. He's not getting away with it.'

'What exactly do you mean? You know him don't you? I think the game's over, Travis. You know much more than you're letting on. Travis . . . ' But he was already climbing into his vehicle and set off down the narrow lanes at a very dangerous rate.

'What's going on, Mummy? I'm scared. I didn't like that man even if he did have a water plane. He said I could go in it one day, but I don't really think I want to anymore. He was horrid. He even kicked poor old Pooch when he was only going to wag his tail at him.

You know how he does. Said 'clear off you mangy beast.' What's mangy?'

'Never mind now, love. I'm just wondering if I ought to go after Travis. Trouble is, I don't know where he's gone.'

'Everything's getting all upset and I don't like it. Why's everyone so cross suddenly?'

'I'm sorry Scotty. It's a rather worrying time and we're not cross with you.'

'Where's Travis gone? Only the timber should get here soon and he won't be here to unload it.'

'Scott, I'm sorry, but I think Travis may have left us. I know it's a bit of a shock but he might have been . . . ' she realised she couldn't bear to say the words out loud. If he had really been working for the enemy, as she thought of Andrews, she didn't want Scott to know.

Besides, she hoped she was wrong and it would be positively slanderous to express her thoughts. 'He might have to work somewhere else. In fact, we might even find ourselves another house. Somewhere that doesn't mean quite so much work for us all. It might be exciting.'

'But this is fun sort of work. I like it here best. You sent Travis away, didn't you? You were talking last night and were cross with each other then. Why did you send him away? I hate you. He's my best friend I ever had.'

'Scott, no. I didn't send him away. Truly. He . . . he just left.'

'Then why didn't he wait to take his stuff? He's left everything and he wouldn't have done that if you hadn't been cross. Maybe he wanted me to have his computer,' he added, brightening up with the sudden thought.

'Oh Scotty. Come here.' She leaned down and drew the child into a warm hug. 'Look, I know you're disappointed. So am I. I like Travis too. I liked him a lot. But not everything is quite so simple when you're grown up.'

'Please ask him to come back.'

'I can try to call him. OK? I'd really like to know why he rushed off like that.'

Lauren dialled his mobile number. Upstairs in his room, they heard his phone ringing.

'That's that then,' she said softly. She wiped away a small tear before Scott could see it.

9

Lauren went back inside, frustrated and anxious. She put the kettle on, needing the curative properties of tea. Her and her big mouth and stupid suspicions. She wanted to believe that Travis was on her side. Why else would he have worked so hard for her? But he was always so secretive about his past and even his present activities. He obviously had money, so what was he doing here in this isolated place? What was his motive? The questions raced round her mind as she tried to get on with her chores.

'There's people here, Mum,' Scott called out.

'We're closed.' But the visitors insisted on coming into the shop.

'We'd like to go over to visit the thermal park.'

'I'm very sorry, but it's closed at

present. We have to do some repair work.'

'You mean to say we've driven all these miles to visit and the blasted place is closed? Really, it's too bad. Why didn't you put out some sort of notice along the road?'

'I'm really sorry, but we've been told we can't land anyone over there until the repairs are carried out. As for a notice, we did put one out in the road.' She peered over to look outside, but the notice had been removed. No doubt dear Mr Andrews had something to do with it.

'We saw nothing. Look, we've come a long way to see this place. Can't you take us over? We'll be very careful.'

'It's more than my licence's worth. I'd be breaking safety rules.'

'Well, clearly you're not interested in doing business. I shall report you. False advertising. You'll be struck off the tourism list. I'll make sure your pathetic leaflets are removed from all the outlets.' The man was furious, but reporting her would make no difference. If she had allowed them to visit the site, she would have been in much greater trouble. They stormed out and went back to their car, cursing angrily and refusing her offer of a free tea to make up for their wasted time.

'More people who are cross,' Scott said unhappily. 'Is everyone in the world going to be cross from now on?' He put his arms round Lauren's waist and they stood hugging each other for comfort.

The shop bell rang again. 'I'm sorry we're closed,' she began.

'This where you want the timber delivered?' asked the lorry driver.

'Thanks, yes. As near the water edge as you can get. We have to take it over to the other side on the boat.'

'Got your work cut out. It's weighty stuff. You got someone to help?'

'I can help,' Scott said valiantly.

'Think you'll have to grow a bit, son. These are long planks and hefty ones at that. OK then. I'd better get started. I'd love a cuppa when I'm done.'

'I'll make sure the kettle's boiling. Thanks.'

It took an hour to offload the planks and the heap took up a lot of the landing space. Lauren wondered how she would ever cope with it all if Travis didn't return. She'd have to get some help from somewhere. Paying for the help was going to be another major worry.

She didn't even know how she was going to pay for the materials, let alone expensive labourers. When he'd finished, she asked the driver about payment, praying that he didn't need it right away.

'It's all paid for, love. Didn't your hubby tell you he'd paid? Settled it all when he ordered it.'

'Thanks. No, he didn't mention it.' She felt greatly relieved but all the same, she'd have to pay it back some time.

There was no sight of Travis for the rest of the day. She and Scott went for a short walk to get some air and exercise Pooch before bedtime. They had supper and Scott went to bed.

She missed Travis. His strength, his sense of humour and his many kindnesses. She missed the long evenings they'd shared and most of all, despite her fears, their growing love, or what she'd believed was something special they shared.

She sat thinking all evening and when she went to bed, she had reached a decision. She would have to put the site up for sale and return to England. It was the only sensible thing to do. Andrews couldn't be the only person who would buy the property. She didn't know why she hadn't thought of it before. If the valley was to be developed, there must be other people interested besides him.

The next morning, she went along the road to visit Mrs Campion. 'You look terrible, love. Haven't you slept?'

'Not much. It's been a really bad time. I've decided I have to sell up and go back to England. I know it seems like admitting defeat, but after so much trouble, I really can't manage any more. What with all the vandalism and trouble, I've got to give up before I'm totally bankrupt. I feel sad for Auntie Gwen's sake but it's all just too much for me.'

'Oh, love. You can't give up. Please reconsider. We've grown awful fond of you and we'd hate to lose you. Besides, we need you to help us fight for this valley. Look, come and have a bite of supper with us this evening. Let's talk it through properly then.'

'It's kind of you, but my decision's made.' A look of anguish crossed Mrs Campion's face.

'But I need to talk to you. Please come tonight. Bring Scott of course. I love that little lad of yours. I couldn't bear to think of you being driven away by some mongrel.' She frowned and looked even more troubled.

'Well, thanks. We'd love to come for supper, but you won't change my mind.'

'You can bring that handsome man of yours as well. What's he got to say about your plans?'

'Travis? Well, I'm not entirely sure what's happening. He went out yesterday and never came back. Oh, I'll take some apples please. Scott loves them and it's nice to have something healthy to feed him.'

'Sure thing, love. But please reconsider. You must. See you around six thirty. Won't be anything special and don't dress up, for heaven's sake.'

Scott was fishing from the landing stage when she returned. The faithful Pooch was sitting beside him. In a desultory way, he tossed his line out and dragged it back. He looked the very picture of unhappiness.

'Shall we take a drive into town?' she asked him.

'If you want. Is Travis ever coming back do you think?'

'I don't know, Scott. Look, I want to go and discuss the possibility of selling this place with one of the agents in town. I think it may be the most sensible thing. You know we talked about it before? Well, I think the time has come to make some sort of decision. Come on. We can't take anyone over to the site anyway and we can't fix the landing stage ourselves. If Travis does come back, he might help us with it and then we shall be able to sell the property.'

Scott burst into tears. 'I want to go back to the time when everything was lovely when Travis came and we took visitors to the site and it was all happy. Please Mummy, let's go back to then.'

'I'm sorry love. We can't always go back. Come on. Dry your eyes and we'll go and have us a nice time in town. Mrs Campion's asked us round for supper. That'll be nice won't it?'

'Not really.'

They spent a rather tedious day wandering round the little town. Rashly, Lauren bought a new toy boat for Scott, one with a remote control, hoping it might cheer him up.

The agent had been less than helpful, claiming that there was no call for properties like hers in the area. Even he managed to look shifty and she began to think the wretched Andrews had been right. He was quite unscrupulous enough to try anything to get his own way. Why was he so determined to ruin her and get it for himself? He must have some reason more than needing a small place like that. It wasn't even as if there was a great deal of land with it. Not enough to make it worth his while to go to such lengths, anyhow.

'Maybe Travis will be back when we get home. Shall we go now, in case?' Scott asked soon after lunchtime.

They drove back but everywhere looked deserted. Lauren looked anxiously at the landing stage and even under the house to make sure nobody had paid an unwelcome visit during their absence. Everything looked normal.

Pooch greeted them happily and she wondered what they would do with the large, friendly dog, if they did have to return to England. He'd hate living in a small house on an estate, even if they did have enough money left to buy anywhere.

Besides, there was the long quarantine he'd have to go through. She hated uncertainty at the best of times. Gloomily, she got herself and Scott ready for supper with Mrs Campion.

'Isn't Jamie here?' Lauren asked in surprise.

'He's had to go away for a while.' She looked distinctly uncomfortable at the mention of her son.

'Oh, dear. You must miss him. He's a great help to you in the store isn't he?'

'Look, there's something I've got to tell you. Oh dear. I'm so ashamed.'

'What is it? Mrs Campion?'

The woman was in tears and looked very upset.

'Look, I don't know how to say this. Jamie and his mates. Well, it was them who did most of this vandal stuff. I nearly killed him when I knew. I could see he had more money than usual and when I tackled him, he flew off the handle and said it was nothing to do with me. Then I overheard him talking to someone on the telephone. Someone from Auckland he said. Business, and I was to stop poking my nose into his affairs. He stormed off out and I did the redial thing on my phone. Some woman answered and said it was some development company. Didn't catch the name. I put the phone down quick.'

'Charles Andrews. Was that the name?'

'I think it was, now you mention it. But, how did you know that?'

'He's been trying to buy my place for weeks. Keeps making ludicrous offers and threatening me. Where's Jamie now? I need him to make a statement to the police.'

'You'll be lucky. He'd end up in jail. He's been in trouble before. I did wonder if it was anything to do with him, this vandal stuff, but I didn't think he'd be so low as to do it to our own folk.'

'But we're not your own folk, are we? We're newcomers. He owes us nothing. Doesn't know us at all, really.'

'But he certainly knew your Auntie Gwen. She was good to him, she was. Gave him odd jobs all the time and made sure he'd always got some sweets to share with his mates. I don't know what went wrong with him. Anyhow, he's gone off. I don't even know where he is now. Just packed a few things and cleared out. I just wish there was something I could do to make it up to you.'

'Get us the supper you promised us. I'm starving.'

'You mean you'll still share a meal with me? After all this?'

'It's hardly your fault. In a strange way, I feel better knowing for sure. Come on. Something smells good.'

Despite everything that had happened that day, Lauren managed to fall asleep. Knowing Jamie was off the scene for a while, she felt slightly more secure, even though Andrews probably had any number of thugs to call on if he needed them. She kept everything locked and the alarms set, just in case.

'Do you think Travis will be back today?' Scott asked for the umpteenth time, next morning.

'He'll probably send for his stuff sometime. I really don't think he will come back. We could go and pack up his things in case somebody calls to collect them. Would you like to help me?'

'Not really. But I suppose I must. Where do you think he might be?'

'I've no idea. He hasn't told us much about his life.'

Every item she picked up, Scott made some comment about when it had been worn or what they had been doing at the time. It was like looking at old photographs when you've lost touch with everyone in them. Some of his things could do with a wash and she decided it would be a gesture she should make. She picked up a load and asked her son to open the door. But he was looking out of the window.

'Mum, there's a water plane thing landing.'

'Oh no,' she muttered. 'Not him again.'

She joined Scott at the window and watched as the plane drew up to the landing stage.

'I want you to stay right out of the way,' she warned. 'Don't speak to him and certainly don't go anywhere near the plane.' But she was speaking to his back as he rushed out yelling excitedly.

'It's Travis. It's Travis in the plane. He's flying it all by himself.'

Lauren felt her heart beginning to thump as she saw the tall figure extricate himself from the plane. He swung Scott high in the air and tucking him under one arm, wriggling and screeching with delight, he strode along the landing stage.

'I see the timber arrived,' he called to Lauren.

'Yes. It came soon after you left. I

had to leave it stacked there.' Her words were disjointed and her throat felt dry as dust. Her knees were trembling as she walked towards him.

'You ready to escape yet?' he asked the still yelling Scott. He set him down and took the little hand that was thrust into his.

'I knew you hadn't left us. Mum thought you had and was getting your stuff packed ready to send on.'

'Whoa there, young man. You thought I'd left you? Left my precious computer behind? Never.'

'Where did you get the plane from?' he asked.

'Well, I have a lot of business to do all over the place, so I reckoned a plane would be a good bet. Some places are difficult to get to and there's usually some water around these parts.'

'You mean it's yours?'

Travis nodded.

'Wow. That's so cool. Can I have a ride in it?'

'If your Mum says it's OK. But not

for a while. We have some serious talking to do.'

'Wow. Cool. Can I go and look at it close to?'

'OK. But you're not to touch anything. Understand?'

The child rushed down to look more closely at this wonder that had arrived in his life and Travis turned back to Lauren.

'Are you OK?'

'I'm not sure. Too much is happening for me to know. I thought I'd ruined everything when you rushed off.'

'Yea . . . what did you mean by the game's over, you yelled after me? You surely didn't think . . . you couldn't believe I was well, working with that toad?'

'I saw your computer. You left it on one day. Leyton Investments? With Andrews' name on your client list? What was I supposed to think? I really do believe you have some explaining to do.'

'Oh Lauren, Lauren. I know I should

have explained myself more, but it was all so difficult. I didn't want to burden you with all my problems and suspicions. Come and sit down. Let me tell you everything.'

'That would be good.'

'Any coffee going? Has there been any more trouble, by the way?'

'No. But I did discover who's been responsible for most of it. Jamie Campion and his mates. Seems Andrews paid them rather well and sheer greed got the better of them. Poor Mrs Campion is devastated. She's been doing all she can to make me stay.'

'What do you mean, stay? You haven't sold out to him have you?'

'Course not. No. I did go to town to see an agent, see what I might get on the open market.'

'And nobody was interested. I guess he's got everyone stitched up. No deals for Emerald Valley or anywhere nearby, except with him. That figures.'

'Seemed that way. But why is he targeting this place? Why here? There must be dozens of much more commer-cial places in the country.'

'Nowhere quite like this. You've said it yourself. It's unique. There are a number of other thermal parks. Bigger ones with more features. But ours encompasses everything.

'We've got the lot. Boiling mud pools, geysers, silicone terraces and cascades. You name it. There are magical colours everywhere and the cave itself is something quite unique.'

'But the park's not for sale. None of it. We can only ever look after the place. So why is he so keen to get my property?'

'He came here once, as a kid. He was from a poor family and some charity brought a group of kids on a camping trip. He thought it was paradise and made a vow that one day, it would all be his.

'Over the years he became successful but only by using many underhand ways of getting what he wanted. Didn't care who he ruined on his way. Believe me, you don't want to know it all.'

'Oh, but I do. And what your involvement is. But go on.'

'OK. He made his first million through drugs dealing. Got people hooked and then made them work for him. He then decided he needed respectability, at least on the face of it. He began his property deals. It's been a good time for property deals over the years.

'Small places bought cheaply and tidied up, were sold at a profit and well, it just grew from there. More and more properties. More profits. He'd do anything to get what he wanted, including his terror tactics. Always managed to cover his tracks so nothing could be pinned on him.'

'But what's this got to do with your finance company?'

'It was my father's company.'

'But . . . you said he was dead? And why is it called Leyton?'

'Dad had named the business for me. Seemed to think Leyton sounded more trustworthy than Travis. Don't ask me why. Dad worked hard and soon got a very respectable client base. He didn't know there was anything shady about Andrews and took him on in good faith. Trouble was, Dad was too honest for such a devious man.

'Andrews was largely responsible for my father's death, in fact. He tried to continue with his dodgy dealing and when Dad called a halt, he was involved in a so-called accident, very soon afterwards.

'He'd been called out to see a client in some remote place. A fictitious client it turned out. He was in a car crash down a steep, lonely road. The car was completely burnt out and no evidence left of anything untoward. I thought the brakes had been damaged, but couldn't prove it.'

'And you think Andrews somehow caused the accident? Oh, Travis, that's terrible.'

'I'm certain of it. But I have no proof of course. Even if he didn't cause the accident and Dad really did lose control as the inquest suggested, I know it must have been the stress he'd brought on Dad.

'It could have affected his driving, made him lose concentration. Andrews was constantly making threats, but always made sure nobody heard him or could tie him in with anything.

'He's too clever for that. He took his money from the business when I took over and closed his account. Fortunately, the business was still viable and now, with better management, it's flourishing well at the moment.'

'I'm still not clear why you came here, Travis. Why did you pretend to be a simple labourer?'

'Because I heard a rumour that he wanted to buy property in this valley. He really does want to develop the area and what he sees as improvements are exactly what will ruin the place. He doesn't see that. I thought that if I was in the area, I could keep an eye on what was going on. I saw your advert and knew it was fate. Think I hit the jackpot, don't you?'

'Oh Travis, I don't know what to think. He'll surely come back won't he? He's hardly likely to give up now.'

'I don't know. I doubt it. Now he knows I'm here and involved, he's afraid I might have something on him. The police already want to ask questions about all sorts of things. If it's true what you say about him paying Jamie to cause so much trouble, maybe we can finally nail him. They've been investigating him for some time now. I nearly caught up with him when I chased him, but he was just a bit too quick for me. That's why I was away so long. I was following up various leads. Forgot my mobile phone too, which didn't help.'

'So we discovered. But I'm still not sure why someone like you would spend so much time labouring for me for no money . . . in fact, I also owe you a considerable sum for timber and everything else.'

'Forget it. Don't you really know why

I'm here? Once I'd seen you, I knew it was precisely where I wanted to be. I love you, Lauren.'

'What? How? What do you mean?' she blustered.

'Quite simple. I fell in love with you almost at once. You and Scotty there. Dare I hope you feel anything for me? Just a little spark that could grow into something larger?'

'Oh Travis, of course I do. I love you. I fell in love with you almost from the start. But you kept pulling away from me. I practically threw myself at you once and you pushed me away. I thought I'd got it all wrong. Misread the signs or something.'

'There's something else you need to know.'

'Not more confessions?'

'Fraid so. I'm married. The divorce is getting sorted, but that's one of the reasons I've had to keep going away. I couldn't allow you close to me until I knew I was really free. It was pretty tough to resist you. Anyhow, Claire has finally agreed, on most unreasonable terms, I might add. But it will be worth it to be free of her crazy demands. So, you won't be getting a wealthy man after all. There's enough to give us a decent life and we'll always have Emerald Valley.'

'Does that mean you'll have to sell the plane?' asked a voice from the doorway.

'Have you been listening?' Lauren demanded.

'Only a bit. It was quite exciting in places. Just like a film. Does that mean you'll get married? And will Travis be my dad?'

'That's up to your mum,' Travis answered.

'Yes please,' she said.

The next few days seemed rather strange with an almost dreamlike quality. Lauren felt a degree of frustration that Travis was still holding back, but was content to know that they would have a future together. It was quite romantic in some ways. He insisted on being truly free before they could actually become engaged.

She used the time to learn more about him and tried to discover what really made him tick.

Despite his protestations that he would no longer be rich once the divorce settlement was paid, she realised that he owned a very successful business and that his personal wealth was far and away more than she could ever have dreamed of.

'Shouldn't we get someone to help with all this work?' she suggested after they'd spent a whole day hauling timber across the lake. 'I know I can't afford it at the moment, but we shall be making money once we're back in business and I can pay you back.' But he wouldn't hear of it.

'I just love doing things with my hands. This is where I'm happiest. This is where I want to spend my life.'

'But what of your business dealings?'

'I have an excellent assistant back in Auckland and with modern technology, I can do most stuff from here. Keep in touch. With that and the occasional trips up there in the plane, I shall manage perfectly. Probably be able to manage everything in one day and be back at bed time.'

'But it's all such hard work.'

'Are you complaining?' he asked.

'Course not. Only it doesn't seem right somehow.'

'Don't know why. I thought it might be good to give the house a bit of a modernise. Put in heating for the winter. Another bathroom or two. And we can add some decent equipment to the café . . . offer better meals instead of just snacks. Take on a few staff.'

'You just can't let anything rest, can you?' laughed Lauren. 'Must be the entrepreneur in you. But, it all sounds great.'

A week later, Travis ran up the path having collected the mail. He was waving an envelope.

'It's here. The divorce papers. I'm free.'

'That's great,' Lauren called back.

'Come here.' She went out and saw he was kneeling on the top step.

'What on earth are you doing down there?'

'Will you marry me? Allow me to be the father of your children? All of them, present and future?' He held out a small box.

'Course I will. You don't need to kneel down there. Get up. Someone might come.' He pressed the box into her hand. She opened it with trembling fingers. 'Oh Travis. It's gorgeous. The most beautiful diamond I've ever seen.'

'Try it on then.' He placed it on her finger and she stared in delight.

'It's wonderful. Thank you. But I'm sure it was far too expensive for me. When did you get it, by the way?'

'When I was away the previous trip. When Claire agreed to settle.'

'And you were so sure I'd say yes?'

'Of course. I saw the way you looked at me . . . you can't deny it. All moony eyes and soppy expression.'

'I did not.'

'Phone's ringing, in case you two didn't hear it,' Scott called.

'Have you been listening again?' Lauren asked.

'Only the last bit. When you were being soppy. Nice ring, Mum. Now, is anyone going to answer this phone?'

Travis leapt up the steps and went inside. He returned a few minutes later, a grin on his face. 'Guess what? They've got him. The police have caught Charles Andrews. They've assembled enough evidence to put him away for years. Apart from the trial, it's all over. Emerald Valley will stay as beautiful as it always was. A few improvements here and there maybe, but nobody will ever ruin our own hidden paradise.' He pulled his new fiancée to him and kissed her, very thoroughly.

'Is this how it's going to be from now on?' Scott demanded. 'Only I think I'd rather have it the way it was before. All this kissin' and stuff. Yuk!'

'Nothing's ever going to stay just how it was before. Life's full of exciting changes,' his mother told him happily.

Other titles in the
Linford Romance Library:

LOOKING FOR LOVE

Zelma Falkiner

Fleur's sweetheart, Tom, disappeared after being conscripted into the Army during the Vietnam War. Twenty years later, Fleur finds a package of his unread letters, intercepted and hidden by her widowed mother. From them, she learns that he felt betrayed by her silence. Dismayed, but determined to explain, Fleur engages Lucas, a private investigator, to help in the search that takes them to Vietnam. Will she find Tom there and put right the wrong?

RELUCTANT DESIRE

Kay Gregory

Laura was furious. It was bad enough having to share her home with a stranger for a month — but being forced to live under the same roof as the notorious Adam Veryan . . . His midnight-dark eyes challenged Laura to forget about her fiancé Rodney, and she knew instinctively that Adam would be a dangerous, disruptive presence in her life. She'd be a fool to surrender her heart to such careless custody . . . but could she resist Adam's flirtatious charm?

CHANCE ENCOUNTER

Shirley Heaton

When her fiancé cancels their forthcoming wedding, Sophie books a holiday in Spain to overcome her disappointment. After wrongly accusing a stranger, Matt, of taking her suitcase at the airport, she is embarrassed to find he is staying at her hotel. When she discovers a mysterious package inside her suitcase, she suspects that the package is linked to him. But then she finds herself falling in love with Matt — and, after a series of mysterious encounters, she is filled with doubts . . .

KIWI SUNSET

Maureen Stephenson

In 1869, dismissed from her employment with Lady Howarth after being falsely accused of stealing, Mairin Houlihan emigrates to New Zealand. There she meets Marcus, the son of Lady Howarth, who had emigrated there to farm sheep. But later, despite her innocence, Mairin is held on remand on suspicion of murder. Marcus tries to help her — but with all the circumstantial evidence against her, how can he? If convicted she will hang. Who had committed this terrible murder?

CHASE A RAINBOW

Fay Wentworth

When Sarah starts a new life as an hotelier in her father's homeland, she stirs up memories and family secrets. What is David, the local fisherman, afraid of — and why does his son Sebastian look familiar? Who is plotting against her? She falls in love with Jed, her mysterious handyman; but this can only bring pain, as he too is running away from another life . . . As pasts and present become entangled, can the heartaches finally be put to rest?

DOWN LILAC LANE

Catriona McCuaig

In 1942, Viney Lucas and her brothers were taken by their mother to live in their grandmother's cottage in Lilac Lane in Wales. A lasting friendship began when Sybil came to live with them. After her father returned home from the war, Viney became tied to caring for him and her brothers, whilst Sybil was free to pursue the nursing career they had both dreamed of. Yet the bonds forged between them growing up in Lilac Lane never weakened.

WHAT HAPPENS IN NASHVILLE

Angela Britnell

Claire Buchan is hardly over the moon about travelling to Nashville, Tennessee for her sister's hen party: a week of honky-tonks, karaoke and cowboys. Certainly not strait-laced Claire's idea of a good time, what with her lawyer job and sensible boyfriend, Philip. But then she doesn't bank on meeting Rafe Cavanna. On the surface, Rafe fits the cowboy stereotype, with his handsome looks and roguish charm. But as he and Claire get to know each other, she realises there is far more to him than meets the eye . . .

GRAND DESIGNS

Linda Mitchelmore

Interior decorator Carrie Fraser cannot believe her luck when she is invited to work at beautiful Oakenbury Hall. Nor can she quite get over the owner of the Hall, the gorgeous and wealthy Morgan Harrington. Morgan is bound by his late father's wishes to keep Oakenbury within the family and have children; and the more time Carrie spends with him, the more she yearns to be the woman to fulfil this wish. But the likes of Carrie Fraser could never be enough for a high-flying businessman like Morgan . . . could she?